John Croumbie Brown

Forestry in the Mining Districts of the Ural Mountains

in Eastern Russia

John Croumbie Brown

Forestry in the Mining Districts of the Ural Mountains
in Eastern Russia

ISBN/EAN: 9783337287030

Printed in Europe, USA, Canada, Australia, Japan

Cover: Foto ©Andreas Hilbeck / pixelio.de

More available books at **www.hansebooks.com**

FORESTRY IN THE MINING DISTRICTS

OF THE

URAL MOUNTAINS

IN

EASTERN RUSSIA.

COMPILED BY

JOHN CROUMBIE BROWN, LL.D., &c.

Medalist of International Forestry Exhibition, Edinburgh, for Works on Forestry.

EDINBURGH:
OLIVER AND BOYD, TWEEDDALE COURT.
LONDON: SIMPKIN, MARSHALL, & CO.,
AND WILLIAM RIDER & SON.
MONTREAL: DAWSON BROTHERS.

1884.

ADVERTISEMENT.

AT a meeting held on the 28th of March last year (1883), presided over by the Marquis of Lothian, while the assemblage was representative of all interests—scientific, practical, and professional—it was resolved:—'That it is expedient in the interests of forestry, and to promote a movement for the establishment of a National School of Forestry in Scotland, as well as with a view of furthering and stimulating a greater improvement in the scientific management of woods in Scotland and the sister countries which has manifested itself during recent years, that there should be held in Edinburgh, during 1884, and at such season of the year as may be arranged, an International Exhibition of forest products and other objects of interest connected with forestry.'

In an *Addendum* to Reports made to the Executive Committee by the Jurors selected to award premiums on Forestal Literature, it is stated:

'The following works are exhibited by Dr J. C. Brown:—

Introduction to the Study of Modern Forest Economy.
The Forests of England ; and the Management of them in Bye-gone Times.

Forestry of Norway.

Finland : its Forests and Forest Management.

Forest Lands and Forestry of Northern Russia.

French Forest Ordinance of 1669 ; with Historical Sketch of Previous Treatment of Forests in France.

Pine Plantations on Sand Wastes in France.

Reboisement in France ; or, Records of the Replanting of the Alps, the Cevennes, and the Pyrenees, with Trees, Herbage, and Bush, with a view to arresting and Preventing the destructive consequences of torrents.

Hydrology of South Africa ; or, Details of the Former Hydrographic Condition of Cape of Good Hope, and of Causes of its Present Aridity, with Suggestions of Appropriate Remedies for this Aridity.

Water Supply of South Africa, and Facilities for the Storage of it.

Forests and Moisture ; or, Effects of Forests on Humidity of Climate.

'The other Jurors regret that Dr Brown, whose services on this Jury have been invaluable, is, in accordance with Rule 6 of the Regulations for the Juries, debarred from competing for award. They desire, however, to record their opinion that his numerous works are deserving of the highest commendation.

' Each of Dr Brown's works is complete in itself, though an integral part of a series of volumes in course of publication designed to familiarise students of Forestry with the applications being made of Forest Economy in different lands; and Dr Brown's personal acquaintance with the systems pursued in most countries of the Continent of Europe has been of special service to the Jury of this class.'

For these works on Forestry a Silver Medal was subsequently awarded by the Executive Committee of the Exhibition.

The following volume is designed, along with others, to supply to British students of Forestry some of the advantages to be obtained from foreign travel.

It is on principle that the form of compilation has been adopted.

JOHN C. BROWN.

HADDINGTON, *20th September 1884.*

CONTENTS.

AUTHORITIES CITED.

ATKINSON, p. 121; BAGNERIS, pp. 31, 38; BARRY, pp. 51, 53, 77,
168, 169; CHRISTIE, pp. 7, 11, 18, 22; CORRESPONDENTS, pp. 80, 100,
124, 130, 134, 136; *Fullarton's Gazetteer*, p. 68; GIBSON, pp. 25, 41;
GUINIER, p. 32; HEPWORTH DIXON, p. 44; *Introduction to Study of
Modern Forest Science*, p. 116; JOSSE, p. 86; *Journal of Science, Metals,
and Manufactures*, p. 97; KIRKSHOFF, p. 86; LANSDELL, pp. 45, 83,
152, 169, 174, 180; MICHIE, p. 179; MURCHISON, p, 69, 71, 72;
OLSHERSKE, p. 30; RUSSIAN *Forest Code*, p. 144; WILKINSON, pp. 54,
153.

FORESTRY IN EASTERN RUSSIA.

———o———

PART I.

RUSSIA WEST OF THE URAL MOUNTAINS.

———o———

CHAPTER I.

JOURNEY FROM ST. PETERSBURG.

In two volumes similar to this information has been given in regard to the forest lands and forestry of Finland* and to the forests and forestry of Northern Russia.† On my return to St. Petersburg from visiting the Saima See in Finland, and subsequently visiting Lake Onega in the Russian Government of Olonetz, in the summer of 1882, a

---

* *Finland: Its Forests and Forest Management.* In this volume is supplied information in regard to the lakes and rivers of Finland, known as the *Land of a Thousand Lakes,* and as the *Last-born Daughter of the Sea,*—in regard to its Physical Geography, including notices of the contour of the country, its geological formations, and indication of glacial action, its flora, fauna, and climate ; and in regard to its Forest Economy, embracing a discussion of the advantages and disadvantages of *Svedjande,* the *Sartage* of France, and the *Koomaree* of India ; and details of the development of Modern Forest Economy in Finland, with notices of its School of Forestry, of its forests and forest trees, of the disposal of its forest products, of its legislation, literature, and forestry.

† *Forest Lands and Forestry of Northern Russia.* Details are given of a trip from St. Petersburg to the forests around Petrozavodsk on Lake Onega, in the Government of Olonetz ; a description of the forests in that government by Mr Judrae, a forest official of high position, and of the forests of Archangel by Mr Hepworth Dixon, of Lapland, of the Land of the Samoides and of Nova Zembla ; of the exploitation of the forests by *Jardinage,* and of the evils of such exploitation ; and of the export timber trade, and disposal of forest products. In connection with discussions of the physical geography of the region information is supplied in regard to the contour and general appearance of the country ; its flora, its forests, and the palæontological botany of the regions beyond, as viewed by Professor Heer and Count Saporta; its fauna, with notices of game, and with copious lists of coleoptera and lepidoptera, by Forst-Meister Gunther, of Petrozavodsk.

B

friend, who was an office-bearer in the British and American Congregational Church, to which I was then ministering, while their pastor was taking a few months' relaxation in England, invited me to accompany himself and his family to the Government of Ufa, abutting on the Ural Mountains, whither they were going to visit a near kinsman ; and he held out as an inducement to me to avail myself of this opportunity to visit the district, that our journey should, if suitable arrangements could be made, be extended to Orenburg, and some distance thence into Siberia, and on our return to Orenburg I should be free to proceed thence by railway direct to Scotland, or at least to any port where I might choose to embark to cross the sea which separates our island home from the Continent of Europe. At the same time another office-bearer in the church refunded to me the whole of the outlay I had made on my trips to Lake Samia and Lake Onega, leaving me free to appropriate the money to meet any additional expense which might be entailed by the long overland journey from Orenburg to the coast.

The hearty sympathy of those to whom I was ministering, and their readiness to aid me in prosecuting my study of forestry, as it is presented in Russia, was very pleasant to me. But, after careful consideration, it appeared to me advisable that I should return to Scotland as soon as the term of my engagement had expired, and I very reluctantly declined the preferred kindness of my friends.

I was acquainted with the condition of forestry in the region in question, and with the way thither, though I had never been there ; and a third member of the congregation, now deceased,* who had spent many years in that

---

* I have met, as have others, with people trying to live a holy godly life, Catholics and Protestants alike, who had a great prejudice against science, a consequence in many cases of the teaching through which they had passed. I have not found this to be the case with members of this congregation ; and I consider it right to say so. I wear a gold watch presented to me well nigh fifty years ago by some of the young men of the congregation and their friends, with the inscription—' To the Rev. John C. Brown, as a mark of esteem from those who have attended his Lectures on Chemistry. St. Petersburg, March 18th, 1840.'

During my residence amongst them in the summer of 1878 one of these young men— a young man no longer, and one who then preferred in worship the liturgy of the

region, engaged in works of engineering, which brought him into an extensive knowledge of the treatment of forests there as this appeared seen from outside the forest service, placed at my service copious notes preserved by him of what he had witnessed, and he was a man of close, accurate, and deep observation ; a Russian nobleman also for whom I have a high esteem, who is the owner of valuable mines and extensive forests in the Government

Church of England to the more simple ritual followed in the British and American Chapel, spent day after day, week after week, translating with me and for me reports and papers relative to forests and forestry in all parts of the empire. And in my residence among them in the summer of 1882 we had periodical botanical lectures and excursions attended by young men and maidens, old men and children, in numbers ranging from twenty to forty on the excursions, and from fifty to eighty at the lectures. In these excursions we visited numerous localities within thirty miles of the city, easily reached by river steamer or other conveyance ; and usually provision of tea and cake for all was made by some member of the congregation, the partaking of which was generally followed by the doxology, sung spontaneously at one of the first gatherings, and afterwards continued :—

> 'Praise God from whom all blessings flow ;
> Praise Him all creatures here below ;
> Praise Him above ye heavenly host ;
> Praise Father, Son, and Holy Ghost.'

And some time after I had got home I received from the secretary of the church a letter, of which the following is a copy :—

' British and American Chapel, St. Petersburg, December 2nd, 1882.

' Dear Dr Brown,—At our monthly meeting held last evening I was directed by the unanimous voice of the church to convey to you an assurance of its gratitude for the services which you so willingly and ably rendered it last summer during the absence of our esteemed pastor.

'The pleasure which I feel in the performance of so agreeable a task would be complete were I not conscious of a sad dearth of terms in which to give expression to the deep sense of obligation towards you under which the church feels itself placed. It does not forget that it owes its existence and its privileges in a great measure to your untiring energy and devoted zeal in the great work of binding together in the bonds of Christian fellowship the members of the Christian church. It also members with gratitude that during its somewhat chequered existence you have remained a true friend and a loving counsellor. It was remarked by one of our oldest members last evening that you built the church. This was a happy metaphor, and it must have occurred to the minds of many present that you had never failed to embrace every opportunity to lend a helping hand towards keeping the church which you built in good repair.

' Your last visit—perhaps more than any which preceded it—has been the cause of heartfelt thanksgiving to Almighty God for His goodness in preserving to the church so trusty a friend and so willing a helper. The record of your prayers, your counsel, and your sympathy, is kept *within* us. The recollection of your visit refreshes and encourages us. It will, perhaps, be a matter of special interest to you to learn that the pains you bestowed in introducing the younger members of the community to the beauties which botany reveals have not been lost ; your happy application, to each individual life, of the truths which nature teaches told upon your audience, and the members of it are grateful to you for opening their eyes to much that is loveable and instructive in the world around them, and which formerly they heedlessly passed by.

' We, as a church, earnestly pray that you may long be spared to continue your labours in the cause of Christ, and for the advancement of learning, that your declining years may be years made bright and joyous by the conviction that you are approaching a haven of rest—rest from trouble, from sorrow, not from work, for

of Ufa, and who had, I knew, sought to have these forests managed in accordance with modern forest science, at my request gave instructions to the agents on his estates to procure for me, and communicate to. me, whatever information in regard to these I might desire to obtain ; and though I was unable to accompany my friends I could, with what I knew of the country and its ways, picture to myself their progress.

> . . . " After Christ, *work* turns to privilege.
> And henceforth, one with our humanity,
> The six-day Worker working still in us
> Has called us freely to work on with Him
> In high companionship." . . .

And against *this work* declining years form no barrier,

> " For age is opportunity no less
> Than youth itself, though in another dress,
> And as the evening twilight fades away
> The sky is filled with stars, *invisible by day*."

' A beautiful thought of Longfellow's this, and one which brings with it a long chain of complex feeling, gratitude, hope, and confidence. May the joy which passeth all understanding be yours now, henceforth, and for ever! Again and again thanking you in name of the Church for all your kindness and help.—I remain, dear Dr Brown, Yours very respectfully,

JAS. A. BEZANT,

Hon. Secretary British American Chapel, St. Petersburg, Russia.

'To the Rev. Dr Brown, Haddington.'

While I record the pleasing and the creditable, I can also tell of the discreditable and the ludicrous. My grandfather, extensively known as John Brown of Haddington, the author of the 'Self-interpreting Bible,' who, with the exception of having been three months at school, was entirely self-educated, was accused before an ecclesiastical court of having acquired his learning through compact with the devil. While the lectures on chemistry, to which reference has been made, were being delivered, two ladies of good social position seriously assured a dinner-party at which they were present, that there was a queer minister at the chapel now, who put a great number of bottles in a circle on a table, and knelt down and prayed to them, while all the people kneeled around him. Happily, after the laugh had been enjoyed, a member of the congregation who happened to be at the party was able to tell out of what this strange story had arisen.

Amongst the Germans of a devout spirit in St. Petersburg, it was said about the same time, that at these lectures I poured 'water into one glass and it was red ; that I poured this into another glass, and it was green ; that I poured this into another glass, and it was blue ; and so on, for a long time ever producing new changes. This, it was alleged, could only be done by the 'black art ;' and Pastor Neilsen, of the Moravian Church, afterwards bishop of the community; was asked to deal with me. I was aware of this ; and, after meeting him repeatedly without his broaching the subject, I said to him one day, 'Pastor Neilsen, have not you got a message for me?' He evidently disliked the commission, but after a little he said : ' My dear brother, I do not believe what some of our friends do ; but seeing that your lectures are occasioning a scandal '—— I stopped him, saying, ' Come to one of our meetings, and after that we will discuss the matter.' He declined, but I insisted, refusing to discuss the matter till he knew what it was. He at last consented, and came to one of our meetings. They were held in my dining-room. At the close of the lecture he came, and taking both my hands in his, said : ' My dear brother, I only wish we could have such meetings among us.'

Their journey took them from St. Petersburg, through Moscow and Nijni-Novgorod to the Volga and the Kama, and thence by land to their destination.

The Moscow railway station in St. Petersburg is situated at the further extremity of the Nevskoi Prospekt, a noble, spacious street, a hundred and thirty feet in breadth, and of proportionate length. It and other two prospekts diverge at equal angles from the central spire of the Admiralty, which, like St. Paul's Cathedral in London, and the Tuilleries in Paris, may be considered the centre of the city.

Beyond the Admiralty, on the one hand, stands the Winter Palace, on the other the Synod-House and the Senate-House; behind is the Neva in its full flow; immediately in front is the Alexandra Sad, formerly known as the St. Isaac Plain, a noble quadrangle, surrounded by noble buildings. I have seen massed on it a hundred and five thousand soldiers, with their entire equipments— infantry, cavalry, and artillery—Russians, Finns, Cossacks, Circassians, and representatives of various Caucasian and Trans-Caucasian tribes; and, according to estimated numbers, ninety-five thousand spectators on surrounding platforms and roofs, the whole being visible from every spot. It was on the occasion of the consecration of a magnificent monolith pillar erected there to the memory of Alexander the First. The effect, when all were hushed, and the quavering voice of the Metropolitan reading the prayers of consecration, came in undulations over the heads of the soldiery, produced a thrill which is even now reproduced as I recall the incident; but a more intense thrill was produced when the whole at one moment rose from the attitude of worship on the conclusion of the prayers—the horsemen raising the bowed head and replacing the plumed helmet, the footmen rising from a kneeling posture. The scene was like unto some of the grosser representations of the expected resurrection, and the pictures formed by fancy of the prophet Ezekiel's vision of the valley of dry bones:—'And there was a noise, and behold a shaking, and the bones came together, bone to his bone, and the breath came unto them, and they lived and stood up upon their feet, an exceeding great army.'

It is fifty years since this occurred ; but I see it again as if it were to-day.   From what has been stated, some idea may be formed of the extent of the plain.   Since then it has been converted into a large landscape garden with magnificent fountains, winding walks, herbs, and flowers, and trees, and flowering shrubs, and an artificial mound, with numerous benches, whence is seen the Neva, and the fortress and the islands beyond ; while even the cravings of little children have not been overlooked : in various places, surrounded with benches, are heaps of clean sand where, as on the beach in Britain, children, under the eye of parents or other guardians, or free from all such control, may play to their heart's content with wheelbarrows, shovels, and buckets, of like tiny dimensions.   This it is which is called the Alexandra Sad, or Alexandra Garden.

Within this is enclosed the famous equestrian statue of Peter the Great, placed on a massive granite boulder, brought thither with great difficulty, and erected to his memory by Catherine the Great ; and outside of the enclosure, at the opposite extremity of the plain, is the pillar of red granite, eighty feet high, surmounted by the figure of an angel and a cross, to the consecration of which to the memory of Alexander the First I have referred.

This stands in front of the Winter Palace, but at such a distance as the great extent of the plain required in order to maintain æsthetic proportions.   The palace, in the winter of 1837-38, had its entire interior destroyed by fire.   I witnessed the catastrophe.   The walls of the palace are surmounted by statues in varied attitudes.   While the flames and smoke, rising high above these, not unfrequently came swirling around them, and at times completely invested them, they looked in the quivering and alternating light and shadow, as if alive and moving—demons directing and joying in the conflagration ; while the angel with the cross, on his lofty pedestal, as the glare of light fell upon him, seemed calmly directing the gaze of the pigmy men below to heaven and God.

The palace, I need scarcely add, was in due time restored to its pristine condition, with superadded adornment.

The Alexandra Garden is immediately in front of the Admiralty. Beyond this, in a corner at one end is St. Isaac's Church ; in the corresponding corner at the other is the *Glavnoi Stab*, or Government offices, facing the palace, with a sweeping curve, in the centre of which is a befitting archway surmounted with a warrior in his war chariot, drawn by six horses abreast, in the attitude of full gallop.

'St Isaac's Church,' writes the Rev. James Christie in his volume entitled *Men and Things Russian ; or Holiday Travels in the Land of the Czar*, 'Standing in one of the largest open spaces in the capital, and surrounded by the finest buildings and monuments, the Cathedral of St Isaac cannot fail to be admired for its grand proportions and simple architecture, and noble porticoes and glittering domes, the loftiest of which can be seen afar down the Neva by the traveller who approaches the Russian capital by the water route. In order to secure a sure foundation for this magnificent ecclesiastical structure, which was commenced in 1819, and took forty years to finish, a whole forest of piles, each of them 21 feet long, was sunk in the treacherous soil at the cost of £200,000. This precaution, however, appears to have been insufficient, for never since the church was consecrated in 1858 has the scaffolding been removed from any part of the building above, the work of propping up the foundations, particularly on the river side, always going on. At present that side is entirely blocked up with timber. The church cost three millions. It is in the form of a Greek cross ; that is it consists of four equal sides. Each of these possesses a principal entrance approached by a broad flight of steps of Finland granite,

while the peristyles are supported by 112 gigantic
polished granite monoliths, each 60 feet high, and having
a diameter of 7 feet.   This massive exterior has for its
counterpart a splendid and costly interior, which somewhat disappoints because of its sombreness during the
day.   This very quality, however, may help to add to its
imposing grandeur when at some festival, beginning as is
usual in the Russian church at the evening service, it is
brilliantly illuminated with some thousands of candles
and tapers.'

Converging towards the central spire of the Admiralty,
are the three prospekts of which mention has been made,
their length being reckoned by miles.   That on the left,
the noblest of the whole, perhaps I should say the only
noble one of the three, is the Nevskoi, considered by some
travellers to be in some respects the finest street in
Europe. I have witnessed successive additions made to the
heights of the houses, by which it has been improved ; but
I have seen the fronts of these houses by degrees covered
more and more, from ground floor to attic, with garish
signboards, greatly marring the effect.   Again and
again the long line of these is broken by bridges,
churches, palaces, public buildings of different kinds,
and palatal and public gardens.   My desire is simply to
give some idea of the appearance of St Petersburg presented to the traveller setting out thence to travel in the
forests and forest lands of the East, and of the Ural
Mountains, and of the far stretching land beyond, extending from the Ural Mountains to the Amoor and Kam-
schatka ; and in order to this I do not deem it necessary
to give details of particular buildings.   Amongst others
there, are the Imperial Library, the Grand Opera, the
Kazan Church, with a façade like that of St Peter's at
Rome, and churches of other forms innumerable, and the
Gostinnoi Dvor, or Market, where may be purchased anything and everything, from a cradle to a coffin, jewels, and
old iron and rags,

At the extremity of this noble street, but still in sight of the spire of the Admiralty, is the St. Petersburg terminus of the Moscow railway, whither the traveller may come from the Alexandra Sad by tramway car. Punctually the train starts; and on the instant numerous hands are in movement, making three times upon the breasts the sign of the cross—the symbol of prayer for a safe conduct—a rite which may have been observed in the tramway car when the Kazan Church, or any other church, was passed; and which may be seen again whenever the train passes within sight of a church. In this particular a great difference may be observed in the departure of a train by the Finnish line, and even the departure of a train by the Warsaw line. In Finland the people are Protestants, and during the summer months many of the passengers in first and second class carriages are Jews or Germans, going to or from their summer lodgings. The Warsaw line conveys passengers not only to Poland, but to the whole of Western Europe. But the Moscow line conveys passengers to all parts of the interior of Russia, and the great bulk of the passengers are Russian; and this is a Russian usage, a usage of which comparatively few Russians are ashamed, and I honour their observance of it.

The train having started, there comes the conductor and two subordinates to check the tickets of the passengers. The carriages are similar to those used in America—the entrances are at the two ends, passing, in many cases, a water-closet for the use of passengers while travelling; and being connected with couplings covered by a bridge, the guards and the passengers alike can freely pass from one carriage to another, and the former from end to end of the train, which they do from time to time, giving to timid passengers a feeling of protection, which such may desiderate in Britain. The uniform of the conductor and guards, as on other lines of railway in Russia, is national. On this line it consists of a hat of Astrakhan black wool, a surtout buttoned to the neck, bound round the waist with a magenta coloured sash ending in long tassels, blue trousers, and long brightly polished boots.

It is said that when the chart representing the line which the surveyors proposed for the railway between the two capitals was submitted to the Emperor Nicolas, he took a pencil and ruler and drew a straight line from the one point to the other, saying, *Kak boodit!* (So be it!) and so it was constructed—not as the professional engineers designed, but as the Sovereign willed it to be; and viewing the railway system of Russia as primarily of importance with a view to military tactics, it may be that the Imperial military projector was right. In consequence of the course followed by the line several towns of importance are passed at a distance; but it passes through the town of Tver, with a population reckoned at 28,000, situated on the Volga. And here the traveller may leave the railway carriage for the steamboat, and embarking, pass over some hundreds of versts of his journey with less fatigue than even that experienced in travelling by railway. But time has a money value, and most travellers for the east and the south who can afford to do so continue their journey by railway to Nijni-Novgorod, and embark upon the Volga there. The country between St. Petersburg and this is very level; it is but poorly cultivated; and it is uninteresting. The line of rails crosses the Valdai Hills, in which the Volga, debouching on the Caspian; the Dwina, flowing into the Black Sea; and the Volkhof, take their rise. My brother, travelling from St. Petersburg to Moscow by diligence, before the days of railways, said one evening to the conductor, 'Please awake me, if I happen to be asleep, when we reach the Valdai Hills.' 'The Valdai Hills!' said the conductor, with a look of astonishment, 'why, we crossed them yesterday!' And, like my brother travelling by diligence, the traveller by railway may cross the entire range without ever remarking a departure from the dead level over which he had previously passed.

Of Moscow it concerns me not here to speak.

By a second line of railway the traveller proceeds from Moscow to Nijni-Novgorod. The lower-lying Novgorod, or Newtown, so named in contradistinction to Novgorod the Great, an ancient capital of Russia.

Nijni-Novgorod is situated at the confluence of the Oka and the Volga, the connecting link of the several chains of lake and river communication whereby produce and goods may be transmitted from almost any part of the empire to any other, and from St. Petersburg to the remote east, from Odessa and Astrakhan to the remote north, and from any of these parts to all places in connection with either of the others.

An annual fair held here has long been famous, and has been spoken of as one of the wonders of the world.

The ground on which the fair is held lies between the railway station and the river Oka. The town lies beyond. From a steep hill, adjacent to the town and the river, may be obtained a birds-eye view of the whole. Mr Christie describing the scene in the volume I have cited, tells :—' Two miles distant there lies the station . . . and at our feet the confluence of the great rivers which bind the whole empire of Russia together in a network of water communication. Across the Oka a bridge of boats is thrown, always crowded with strangely heterogeneous specimens of humanity, and joining the town to the fair. On the bosom of this river there float scores of steamboats, and curiously constructed barges, a number of them capable of carrying a freight exceeding eight hundred tons. The present destination of many of these craft is Moscow, and the far-distant interior of Russssia, whither they are carrying the treasures of the distant East, while those now descending the river are bringing to the fair the notions of the West for the bazaars of the East. At right angles to the mouth of the Oka there flows the mighty Volga, the Mississippi of Russia, by no means a silent highway during the holding of the fair. Even now in summer, it is a broad stream, and ever widening the farther you descend, to the eye's delecta-

tion; but after all, at this season, it is only an attenuated
thing compared with what it will be in spring, when, with
the melting of the snows and rains, it swells, and swells,
and overflows its banks, and inundates thousands of
square miles in the different provinces through which it
flows, leaving behind it, as it retires, a rare residue of
fever and ague,—for a season, the terror of all eastward-
bound travellers, and the *bête noire* of the peasants who
dwell upon the littoral. This noble river, which has
already run a long course, and has still fourteen hundred
miles to flow before it empties its waters into the Caspian
Sea, is at present literally crowded with barges and steamboats, and the Volga now carries upwards of six hundred
steamers on its bosom. There they are, from Astrakhan,
and the Caspian, and Kazan, barges that have sailed
down the rivers of Siberia and the noble Kama, to lay
the produce of the frozen North and of the Urals at the
feet of the merchants of Europe assembled for trade
purposes at Nijni-Novgorod. These busy rivers are in
themselves sights not to be forgotten; but after all, the
sight *par excellence* is the fair itself, and thither accordingly we wend our way. Once across the bridge of boats,
we are into it at once, or more accurately into it and a
cloud of dust. This last is easily accounted for. Once
that the fair is officially closed, all the booths and ware-
houses are locked up, the merchants leave as fast as they
can get away, and the residents in the locality, having
transferred themselves and their belongings to the town
proper, the fair is left to rats, and mice, and solitary
policemen. What becomes of the rats and mice at a
later season, which is also an earlier, for it is the spring I
speak of, deponent knoweth not, but at that season the
quiet and tenth-rate dressed guardians of the peace must
leave their solitary beat, for when the Oka and Volga
overflow their banks, the vast plain on which the fair is
built is covered with muddy water, to the depth of never
less than fifteen feet. Granted, then, the fierce summer's
sun, and the incessant tramping of many thousands of

feet, and it is easy to account for the plague of dust which rises, and hangs in the air, and clogs the air-passages, and powders the sober costume of Western tourists until their dearest friends would hardly know them again, or at least would inquire, could they only see them, " Have you been transmogrified into the lineal descendants of the Miller of the Dee ? "

' At one end of the bridge of boats there stands the Exchange, a poor though large wooden structure ; and here thousands of traders will assemble every day, and effect transactions during the fair to the tune of millions. And then at once, and immediately beyond the Exchange, begin the rows in which the different commodities are stored.   A broad and deep canal in the shape of a horse-shoe separates the inner rows, situated in the vicinity of the Governor's house, from those in the more outlying districts.   This is a precaution against fire.   In the bazaar proper, and in the booths of the merchantmen, many different nationalities are represented.   A few Englishmen, and no end of Germans ; Russians innumerable, as is natural ; Tartars by the thousand, some of them dealers in fancy-coloured boots and scull-caps, and many of them servants and porters—in fact, the hewers of wood and drawers of water to the fair; Circassians, wonderfully subdued-looking when they are in civil life ; and swarthy, tall-hatted Armenians, those Jews of the East, who are even a match for the seed of Abraham according to the flesh, and whose belts never know what it is not to be well lined with bank notes and acceptances. I saw only one native of the land of Sinim.

' It takes a day's hard work to visit the rows, and get a fair notion of the varied contents of the fair, and that work I did until my rebellious feet cried, " Hold ; enough !" —There they were, the tea rows, containing innumerable chests of that great Russian favourite : Captain Rickard informed me he had sometimes bought upwards of 16,000 roubles' worth of tea and sugar at one time at the fair, for the use of the peasants on the estates he manages

down in Orenburg. The rows of the furriers, where, as is
proper in Russia, the peltry is so magnificent, that if
English ladies could only get there with their husbands,
these lords of creation would find they were in for an
awkward quarter of an hour of it. The braziers' rows,
resplendent in samovars, the tea-urns of Russia, mostly
made in the workshops of Tula, on the banks of the Oka,
which have become so fashionable in aristocratic circles in
this country, since the Czar's most able and noble
daughter has become a member of the Royal Family of
England. The china rows, where the most ravishing
pottery and glass-work is displayed. I entered one of the
shops in the china row, and selected a few small and
beautiful articles to bring home with me. Quite incidentally, I asked the salesman where they were made, when I
was getting out my purse to pay for them. To my
astonishment he said " England." " England ! " thought I,
" then it is not worth while carrying coals to Newcastle,"
and telling him I was " Anglichanin," prayed to be
excused from completing the purchase. He smiled, and
graciously acceded to my proposition. Trunkmaker's
rows, filled with many-coloured boxes with bright metal
bindings. These trunks are quite an institution of the
country. Every peasant, man and woman, aims at being
the happy possessor of one of them, in which he can store
up his little " all," and still leave room for more.
Drysalters', paper, cloth, cotton, and linen rows, in which
goods are stored up, sufficient, you would say, to supply
all Russia and the East, and leave much over; but so
great is the demand this year for everything, that before
the two flags are taken down which float at the sides of
the Votive Church, and whose removal indicates the
closing of the fair, every ounce by weight, and every yard
by measurement, will have been disposed of. Fish rows,
in which hundreds of tons of dried sturgeon, and sterlet,
and fish of every kind, and caviare—to eat which with
enjoyment, requires, in my opinion, a developed taste—
are all exposed for sale. Mountains of grindstones for

Russia's innumerable windmills, the very sight of which is more than enough to put the nose of the Newcastle grindstone out of joint for ever; and along the banks of the Volga, for no less a distance than six miles, heaps of iron from Siberia, the finest that the world can produce. We exhaust ourselves with the work of inspection, and when all is over, and it is time to return by the night express to Moscow, the tenth has not been seen.

'It is estimated that fully half a million traders visit the fair during eight weeks, and the estimate cannot be very far wrong, according to all reports. Curiously enough, the estimate is taken from the quantity of bread consumed, the Government compelling the bakers to send in a return each morning of the amount of bread they sell. The money exchanging hands during the fair exceeds £16,000,000 sterling. I travelled from the fair to Moscow in the company of a German Jew, a wholesale St Petersburg store-dealer, who had purchased 84,000 roubles'—upwards of £9000—worth of Siberian rags for purposes of paper manufacture. The purchases are in many cases so large that credit for twelve months, and in some instances for two years, is asked for, and given. In the case of large dealers, the rule is to pay at one fair for what was bought the previous year. It is generally supposed that the gradual extension of the railway system must in time lessen the influence of this gigantic fair; but it is very evident that it will be many years before the glory of Nijni is a thing of the past. This year the trade has been immense, and as the Russian merchants have had it all to themselves, just as they had in the year after the Crimean war, their rejoicings are unbounded. Three hundred millions' worth of goods in roubles were brought forward, and by the middle of August one hundred and eighty millions had been sold. The consequence was, that the fair would close earlier than usual, and with stocks of goods cleared out, the manufactories will have a prosperous year to look forward to.

' Smoking is rigidly prohibited within the bounds of the fair proper, and until within the last two or three years, any one inadvertently breaking the law on this point, by smoking a papiros or cigar, was at once pounced upon by a Cossack or policeman, and mulcted on the spot to the tune of fifty roubles. Without thinking what I was doing, I took my papiros with me into the street as I left the restaurant where I had been dining, when the instantaneous reminder of the policeman caused me to fling it into the canal with certainly greater haste than decorum. This precaution is not unnecessary. Most of the rows, or lines, as they are called, being constructed of wood, one single fire in the fair proper might endanger the whole. The fire-towers are numerous, and, as usual, the watchmen are always on the outlook. The sanitary arrangements are admirable: a perfect system of stone-built sewers has been constructed, and they are flushed with water from the river twice each day. As the bulk of the Russians are great smokers, it is a common thing for the merchants to descend the round towers leading to the sewers from time to time, and enjoy a quiet papiros.'

In many accounts which have been given of the fair by tourists are saddening accounts of the immorality practised during the fair—falsehood, dishonesty, unchastity, and intemperance. Beyond this mention of the fact I do not feel called on to give details.

When I was resident in Russia the booths at the fair were constructed of wood. They were left from the close of one fair till the close of another. Thus they were secured for the following year's gathering; and the merchants knew what accommodation they had secured for goods at the following year's fair. In 1837 a few friends with whom I was associated sent upwards of 50,000 tracts and books, besides copies of the Scriptures in different languages, for sale at the fair; these were all disposed of by sale or barter; and it was afterwards dis-covered that part of them were sent by the purchasers to

smaller fairs in various places, and were thus more extensively distributed over the empire. I make mention of
this because of the opportunity which doing so affords for
giving a brief illustration of the way in which business
was carried on then, and probably is still. A booth was
hired by the friend entrusted with the work. Here his
books were displayed for sale. He was well acquainted
with Russian modes of dealing, and thoroughly acquainted
with the Russian language in so far as it was used in
trade and commerce. In answer to the question, ' What
have you got here ?' He showed his stock. In answer to
the offer ' I'll take a thousand if you will take pocket
handkerchiefs in exchange,' he might say, ' I shall do so for
half the amount of the purchase money if we can agree
on terms;' and thus one bargain might be made. To the
next inquirer he showed his books and pocket handkerchiefs ; and in his sale to him he might dispose of one half
of the pocket handkerchiefs, and 500 tracts and books, for
cash and a quantity of logwood. To a third inquirer he
would show books, pocket handkerchiefs, and logwood.
And proceeding thus he had so to order his bargains as to
get the whole of his original stock disposed of, and the goods
taken in exchange disposed of for others which could be
sold in St. Petersburg, or exported if they were not such.
On this occasion there passed through his hands in the
course of these transactions, besides pocket handkerchiefs
and logwood, amongst other things which I have forgotten,
a horse, a quantity of feathers, and a quantity of quills.

The skill of the salesman is manifested in never taking
anything in barter for which he may not be able to find a
purchaser, and in never taking anything at too high a price.
If he can he will make a profit on every transaction ; but
what he relies on is making a profit on the sum of the
transactions. In our case we were less desirous of a profit
than of avoiding any loss, and securing a wide distribution for our books. We knew beforehand that our books
would be sold at an exhorbitant profit. But this would
be done in localities to which we could not ourselves gain

C

access ; and the higher the price which might be paid by
the ultimate purchaser, the more likely would he be to
value highly his purchase.

From Nijni Novgorod the journey was prosecuted by
steamers on the Volga.

The Volga shows a broad expanse of water and a rapid
current. In twenty-four hours after leaving Nijni, as the
town is curtly designated, the steamer reaches Kazan, 254
miles below, but a much longer time is taken by the
return voyage against the current. It is luxurious voy-
aging. There are steamers built like those on the large
rivers of the United States in America, and others
fashioned after the model of the sea-going steamers of
Europe. In all the fares are moderate, and the fare good,
while at every stopping-place there are crowds of people
offering for sale cooked provisions of various kinds, cold
roasted fowls, boiled eggs, fish-pies, and bread and cakes
of different kinds. The passengers are of all grades.

Again I avail myself of the more graphic pen of Mr
Christie. In writing of his voyage from Nijni Novgorod
he tells :—

'Pursuing our course down the Volga, we may now
take a look for a few minutes at some of our fellow-
passengers. Seated on the upper deck at sunset, drinking
in the wonderful effects on river and land, three Tartars—
the Tartars are Mohammedans—mount one of the paddle-
boxes, and, spreading out their rugs, say their evening
prayers. One of them is an old man, another is middle-
aged, and the third is a youth. The old man is grave—
his faith is supreme with him ; the middle-aged Tartar
wears a look of nonchalance—he takes to his devotion as
a matter of course ; the youth is agile in all his move-
ments, and full of self-satisfaction. A fine-looking lad, it
is a pleasure to see him. Facing towards Mecca, the three
make their salaams, and then falling upon their knees,
perform their devotions Sometimes they lie prone on
the rug, with the face touching it. This lasts for a

quarter of an hour, and then, taking both hands, and rubbing them over the face from the forehead downwards, they rise, fold up their rugs, and go down again among the steerage passengers. At sunrise they again mount the paddle-box, and go through the same exercise. If a great many professing Christians were only one-hundredth part as attentive to the exercises of religion as these Mohammedans, it would necessarily follow, from the nature of their faith, that it would be much better than it now is, alike for themselves and Christendom. These men are a small trading company, who, having finished their business at the fair, are bound for the remote East. And here is another trader—he also is a Tartar, and well, not to say splendidly, dressed. This man comes, he tells us, from Siberia, and he has been to the fair selling his parcel of pelts. The market, he says, has been very good, but sables will hardly sell, the fur of the silver squirrel being all the rage. There are any number of ordinary peasants on board, honest-faced Russians, clad in the long sheepskin coat with the wool inside. It is a general thing to laugh at the Russian peasants because they wander about in sheepskins, but for my part I never saw anything in this dress except to admire. I frequently thought how the poor, and often badly clad English labourers in some parts of our country would envy the Russian peasant his sheepskin coat, if they only saw him in it. Why, with an ordinary covering for his head, and long boots, and the coat, he might set up at once for a gentleman! Nor was the thought foreign to me, that if I should ever have to live in Russia over a winter, and was unable to purchase a set of furs, I should, in spite of any laughter at my singularity, take at once to the sheepskin as a duck takes to water.

'Coming so closely in contact with these Russian peasants, of course you try to catch the idea conveyed by their countenances. And this we do, acting upon the principle, that it is always right to try and get the best, and not the worst, out of a man. When the Greek

sculptor went abroad in search of a model, he went to
discover beauty, and not to search out defects, and he
often found the eye, or mouth, or nose, of beauty, in faces
otherwise homely enough. Unlike the Greek sculptor,
the modern critic (and traveller too, for that matter) very
often goes about in search of something to find fault with.
So far as we are concerned, we have not a single atom of
sympathy with this sort of thing. With all the homeli-
ness, then, and rudeness of the outline of the Russian
peasant's countenance, the idea you get from it is that of
"rest" and "gentleness," things most beautiful and
excellent in themselves, upon which, no doubt, the education his children are sure to receive will improve. They
are a quiet and soft-speaking people, taking an occasional
turn at the "tantrums," in way of relief, just as quiet and
soft-speaking people in other countries sometimes do.

' Here are also a number of soldiers, bound for some
remote military station, and having charge of a number
of huge bales, with the Red Cross badge sewed on them,
belonging to that beneficent guild. Poor fellows! they
are poorly clad, and miserably nourished; if they were
only meat-fed like their English *confrères*, they would be
a little less high in the bone, and upon the whole good-
looking men. We spoke to two of them, and asked a few
questions. When engaged on extra duty, like the
present, they received ten kopecks a day, just about two-
pence-halfpenny, and on that they had to live, or rather,
let us say, exist. We gave one of them some silver
money, and his gratitude was profuse. Captain Rickard
asked him what he would do with it. "Oh," said he, "I
shall go first and have 'Tchi,'"—that is, a few glasses of
tea. I gave another soldier half-a-dozen apples; he
received them with open arms, went to his haversack and
pulled out a piece of black bread, and having sprinkled a
pinch of salt over it, sat down, crossed himself thrice,
saying grace, and had, what was to him, and indeed to
any unfastidious person, a hearty meal. When all was
consumed he crossed himself again, thus giving thanks.

The attention of the Russian peasants to these little pro-
prieties of religion is something very marked, and
exceedingly beautiful.   Now and again, when travelling,
you come across a squad of workmen, say half-a-dozen in
number, preparing to sit down to dinner on board a barge,
or on land.   There is a huge black iron pot, the "yitling"
of the North of England, before them, filled with cabbage-
soup, and small bits of meat, or fish-soup.   Standing
round the pot in a circle, they cross themselves, and then
sitting down partake of their frugal meal, taking along
with it large hunks of black bread, with the utmost propriety.   The foreman takes the first spoonful, and then
lays it down, the others take their turn, and this is
repeated until the pot is emptied, and the fish-bones
picked as clean as fish-bones can be picked, when all of
them rise, cross themselves, and after a little rest are
ready again for work.   The Volga boats call at a number
of stations, and at all of them wood is brought on board
to fire the engine.   This work is invariably done by
women, who certainly have no sinecure.   At these stations
every variety of edibles, and simple drinkables, including
"quass," a fermented liquor made by steeping black bread
in water, is to be had in great abundance.   The peasants
line the landing-stage with their different commodities,
chickens and ducks ready cooked, fish also cooked—
although no true Russian will ever object to eat raw salt
fish : it is a wonder they do not get an attack of diarrhœa,
—apples, nuts, beautiful bread, white and black, gherkins,
cucumbers, and milk.   I several times bought a champagne bottle filled with delicious milk, bottle and milk
costing only ten kopecks.   A number of the river passengers in Russia supply themselves with food at these
landing-stages, and thus, it is needless to say they are
able to live very cheaply.'

In spring the river is full, filled with the product
of melted snow.   In mid-summer and autumn it is less
abundantly supplied with water, and sand banks render

the navigation somewhat tortuous; occasionally the poll
has to be used, and occasionally the steamer may stick
fast for a time.

Mr Christie, in continuation of his narrative, tells:—
'There is no particularly fine scenery on the Volga. The
left bank lies low, and in spring is inundated for miles
inland; on the right bank there is·an occasional bluff,
with some small town or village nestling at its foot, and
then beyond it the far-stretching córn lands. It would
repay any traveller, however, to take a sail down and up
the Volga, if it were only to see the effects of sunrise and
sunset. It is impossible to describe them, nor can these
glorious and glowing heavens be compared to anything,
than to that which the beloved John saw in vision when
he says, "And I saw as it were a sea of glass, mingled
with fire." Together with the splendour of the Volga
sunset, there are the delicious odours borne on the wings
of the evening wind, which rival the perfumes of Araby
the Blest. They seem to the sense to come from many-
acred fields of harvested wheat, and meads of honeyed
flowers. And if day has its life scenes, and the evening
hour its witchery and sweetness, night on the Volga is
not without its wonders. Not without, indeed! Why,
it is full of awe, and wonder, and glory. In returning
from Kazan two nights have to be spent on the river.
On one of them our boat stuck fast, and as there was a
great deal of noise going on I went on deck, in spite of
the river-damp, against which travellers are warned, to
see what was the matter, and lo! what a sight was that
which in a moment burst upon my astonished eyes! The
midnight heavens were all aglow with untold myriads of
large, and lustrous, and liquid planets. The *via lactea*
was the milky way indeed. The stars seemed to come
close down upon you, and you felt as if He, that Wonderful and Almighty One, who made the ordinances of
heaven, the Pleiades with their sweet influences, Orion
with his bands, who brings forth Mazzaroth in his season,
and guides Arcturus with his sons, was very near at hand.

Nor, may I say, did I ever before seem to realise so well as now, the meaning of these inspired words, "And the Lord brought Abram forth abroad, and said, Look now toward heaven, and tell the stars, if thou be able to number them. And he said unto him, So shall thy seed be. And he believed in the Lord; and he counted it to him for righteousness." In this country the stars never can shine with such unparalleled splendour as they do in the high latitudes of Russia.'

Of the Volga it is said that it has the longest course— and, with the exception of the Danube, the largest body of water of any river in Europe. It rises, as has been intimated, among the Valdai hills in Lake Setinger, in lat. 57° N., long. 53° 10', at an altitude of 550 feet above the sea level, and takes a direction in general to the eastward, but with many windings, until it reaches the city of Kazan. The rivers that flow into it above Kazan are, if we except the Oka, of second-rate magnitude. At some distance below Kazan the Volga receives the waters of the Kama, drained from a very great extent of country. It now flows southward with a great volume of water, and it forms the boundary between Europe and Asia for several hundred miles, till, reaching Tzarystyn, it turns east, approaches the Caspian, and after separating into a number of branches, estimated at from 60 to 70, discharges itself into that sea, nearly 70 miles below Astrackhan. Its course is computed at 2,700 miles, and the area of its drainage at 400,000 square miles.

The vast extent of country through which it flows being in general level, it is navigable throughout after passing Tver in the early part of its course. In May and June its waters, receiving great increase from the melting of the snow and ice, the boatmen take advantage of the increased depth to descend its current and avoid those shallows and islands which in other seasons obstruct their course.

From the vicinity of Tver a communication is opened to the Msta, a river flowing north to the Neva.

The principal rivers which flow into the Volga are the Tvertza, the Mologa, the Sestra, the Soscha, the Oka, the Sura, the Kasanka, the Kama, the Sok, and the Samara.

If the expression *the highway of the sea* be justifiable, these rivers may be spoken of as the highway of the desert, both in reference to the conveyance of travellers and to the transport of merchandise, inclusive of the products of the forests. And the Kama supplies to us the means of prosecuting our journey eastward with ease and comfort.

This was the course taken by the friends who had invited me to accompany them on their vist to their kinsman in Ufa.

The Kama rises near Lip, in the Government of Viatka, on a branch of the Ural chain, flows north north-east, south-west, and west through this Government and that of Perm, becomes the boundary between the Government of Viatka and those of Perm and Orenburg; and entering the Government of Kazan, it flows into the Volga on its left bank, after a course of about 1000 miles. It is navigable for boats of light draught (150 poods burden, 6000 lbs. Russian, 5,400 avoirdupois) throughout a great part of its course. Its waters are at the lowest in August, when its depth at Perm is 23 feet 4 inches less than in spring.

The principal affluents of the Kama are the Vichera, the Tshussovara, the Bielaya, and the Ik, on the left bank, and the Olva, Ij, Viatka, and Micka, on the right. The Bielaya, or White River, is turbid, and its waters are of a whitish colour. It rises in the Government of Orenburg, in the Ural chain, to the north-east of Vershni-Uralsk, and after a course of 650 miles flows into the Volga on the left bank, passing in its course Sterlinatamak and Uka.

The Ufa also rises in the Ural mountains, and, flowing through a mountainous and fertile country, after a course of 350 miles, it falls into the Bielaya, near the city to which it gives its name. This was the next stage of the contemplated journey of my friends. It is a city of

10,000 inhabitants, the capital of the Government of Orenburg. It was built in 1573 by Ivan Vassiliwitch to collect the tribute of the Baskirs, and to serve as a barrier against the inroads of the Kirghiz. It is alleged that there was anciently upon this spot a great Tartar city, the capital residence of the Khans of the Nogais.

The site of Ufa is intersected by numerous torrents and ravines. It was once fortified, but the works have been allowed to fall into decay.

The kinsmen whom my friends had gone to visit resided at Bogoyavlensk and Verchotov, both situated in the district of Sterlinatamak, in the Government of Ufa. One of the party wrote to me from on board the steamer when they had reached the vicinity of Ufa.

' Much as we should have liked that you had accompanied us, it is a constant theme of thanks to our heavenly Father that you were prevented. The run to Nijni by rail was tolerable, though at times we were uncomfortably crowded. The great fair of the world was in full operation, but we were too tired to notice anything, and had no guide; we therefore drove directly to the steamboat pier and secured places. The steamer of the Sounolet Company (there are four or five others competing, many grander in appearance, but they could take us only as far as Kazan, therefore we refused) was very comfortable. We got two cabins for two persons each, and one in the general room. The voyage down the Volga was interesting mainly from its novelty, but generally tiring by its monotony. One bank is high, the other low—both alike sand—by no means thickly wooded, excepting in places. The river is wide, and would be noble-looking were it not for the numerous sandbanks. The course of the river itself is tortuous, and the distance the steamer has to run must be extraordinary compared with the measurement by map, for we often seemed to go from one shore to the other, hug it for a few hundred yards, and

then back to the first shore. All this was to avoid running
aground ; and this frequently caused no little excitement, as
three other steamers were in close company, and we had
a captain on his first trip, dependent on his steersman for
everything, and yet of course on his dignity, as master of
the vessel, and naval officer into the bargain.

'We have also experienced this, one of the disagree-
ables of Volga travelling in autumn when water is low,
having, in a narrow and very shallow channel, run aground
in trying to pass another steamer already in that predica-
ment. Tugs refused to help us on the plea that their own
barges were aground, and they ended by driving these barges
firmer on the shallows to save smashing us, of which
the danger was not small ; and the tug also ran aground
so near us that we were nicely fixed, and had to wait till
all obstructions were cleared away before we could attempt
to move. In the end the same tug pulled us off, as he could
not get at his barges while we were in the way.

'The next morning found us safely at Kazan, and having
six or seven hours to wait we climbed the steep bank,
waded about half a verst ankle deep in fine sand under a
tropical sun, and then took train into the town, a distance
of seven versts. This proved too much for my wife,
caused an illness from which she has not yet fully·
recovered, and resulted in her coming home without having
seen anything beyond what was seen in a daily ride taken
towards the end of her visit.

'Having changed vessels at Kazan, we proceeded one
station down the Volga, as far as Bogorodsk, and then
soon turned into the Kama, up which we proceeded as far
as Piavy Bor, and a few versts beyond that pier directed
our course eastward, along the Bielaya. Of the three
rivers I consider, from observation made, but more from
communications by fellow passengers, the Kama by far
the most important, and also the finest river. As on the
Volga, the banks are frequently overgrown with willows of
small size ; but for many versts in extent there were forests
of pine, fir, birch, and other trees. Among others, in the

Menzelinsk district of the Ufa Government, and on the banks of the Kama, a splendid forest was pointed out to me as being in fact the finest collection of timber in the district, and the forest which Prince Lieven returned to the State, on finding that illegal and oppressive measures had been used in giving him the land. Probably you have heard details of the affair, which created some commotion at the time, but which was referred to by my fellow-traveller very sneeringly, as if the existence of pure Christian principles were an impossibility.

'The Bielaya is well wooded on both banks. As far as I could see there are not many large trees near the river, but there are extensive forests of fine trees—fir, oak, elm, birch, willow, aspen, lime, and some others of which I do not know the English names; and I have no dictionary with me.

'The distances travelled by water, according to the time-tables issued by the Steamboat Company, are as follows:

Left Nijni,	Tuesday, 11 A.M.		
Arrived Kazan,	Wednesday, 7 A.M.,	381 versts.	
Left Kazan,	Wednesday, 2 P.M.,		} Volga.
Arrived Bogorodsk,	Wednesday, 5.30 P.M.,	73 versts.	
Arrived Piavy Bor,	Thursday, 9 P.M.,	371 ,,	Kama.
Arrived Ufa,	Saturday, 11 A.M.,	576 ,,	Bielaya.
	Total, 934 miles,	1401 versts.	

'The steamers are very comfortable, attendance fair, food good, and the whole trip from Nijni to Ufa inexpensive—considerably below your estimate per day or mileage.

'Before leaving this part of the journey, I must mention that there is much to interest geologists, especially on the Kama, but my knowledge is too limited, and I do not even know what to call a mass of light grey stone I noticed yesterday, very porous—in fact, like the so-called rockwork we sometimes use in gardens. In other places the displacement of the strata by upheaval is very marked, and to the scientist would be highly interesting. I was struck also, both on the Volga and the Kama, to see how the high bank was frequently cut through by gullies and ravines, evidently the result of the spring torrents.'

Of the land journey my friend subsequently wrote to me:—'At Úfa (pronounced Oofáh) we found two tarantasses awaiting us, We packed in our luggage, bought some bread to prevent starvation, and started to the merry sound of the bells. I had had no experience in packing these conveyances, consequently we had miserable seats; and the hundred versts, under a broiling sun for some hours, and then in darkness till the moon lent its kindly light, gave us no favourable impression of this mode of travelling. No inns providing refreshment exist: such a mark of civilization we left behind us in the town of Ufa; all we could get was the samovar, with cups and glasses, and we used the tea, sugar, &c., &c., we carried with us. Even this was a boon of which we availed ourselves only twice; and we reached Bogoyavlensk works at 1 A.M., famished as hunters, and fatigued almost beyond endurance.

'The Lord's Day was literally a day of rest; for body and brain were alike incapable of any exertion. The younger members proved the strongest, and recovered sooner than I did; but my wife was ill, and scarcely left the house during a fortnight. I recovered soon, and applied myself energetically to fly-fishing, astonishing both the natives and the fish, except when I aimed at the higher game, a species of salmon, when I was thoroughly disappointed. This lasted ten days, and then my brother-in-law and I started for the mines and Orenburg. The first journey was to be 270 versts. We started fairly well, went 50 versts by bye-road, and reached Sterlitamak. There we had food and a little siesta while the sun was too high; we then entered upon the post road, planted during Catherine II.'s reign with a double row of birch trees, which are now in splendid condition, affording an agreeable shade wherever available. I use the term advisedly, for the drivers uniformly begged permission to use a side-road, because the post road was in a condition unfit for travellers.

As for the beautiful alley, it has not escaped the ruthless hand of man, for over the whole extent of a large farm, many versts along the high road, not a single one of the noble trees remains.'

Of the journey from Ufa to Bogoyavlensk a lady of the party wrote to me:—'The journey from Ufa to Bogoyavlensk was made in two tarantasses, to each of which were harnessed three horses abreast. It is pretty hilly, and the roads very good. The first village that we stayed at was a Mahommedan one—rather strange-looking people the Tartars are, especially the women. Bogoyavlensk is an exceedingly pretty place. Eddie and I often made little tours together on horseback. The village seems to be built on a plain surrounded by hills; the latter have vast forests on them, stretching for miles on miles. The river Usolka flows along by the side of the village. About four versts from Uncle Edward's place are the salt springs : to go to these salt springs used to be our favourite drive, the road being so good and the scenery so lovely. We picked up a great deal of ore from the ground. About eighty versts from this place is the village of Vergator. My brother and I went there; and though I had heard much to the disparagement of the scenery there, it pleased me just as much as that at Usolka. The village at Vergator is, perhaps, not quite so prettily situated, but the hills are just as high and the forests just as dense as at the other place. I remarked a great many very beautiful willows on our way—I have never seen such splendid willow trees as those. At Vergator once, my uncle, my brother, and I went out on horseback, the children accompanying us in wagons, for a picnic. We went up to the top of one of the highest hills, where we had the samovar and tea. Below us on one side was a splendid forest, on the other side were stretched different fields of corn, oats. and barley. Between these fields and another forest were two or three streams winding in and out; I cannot describe it properly; but it was simply beautiful.'

CHAPTER II.

IN many parts of Russia we meet with forests consisting almost exclusively of some one kind of tree; and to the student of forest science indications are afforded of the existing state of forests in this particular in special terms which are in use, descriptive and applicable exclusively to different kinds of forests thus constituted. It was so formerly in France, where in old treatises we read of a *chesnaie*, an *aulnaie*, a *urnaie*, a *boulnaie*, a *possellnière*— terms which fell into disuse there when the forests came to be composed of a mixture of different kinds of trees referred to in these designations. But the usage still prevails in Russia where a forest of firs is called *pichtovnikk ;* a forest of birches, *bereznikk ;* a thick forest upon a marsh, *luiva ;* a forest in a hollow, *debre ;* a forest of pines and birches, situated in a sandy country, *borr;* one composed of lofty trees, *doubrava ;* and many such terms are in use, showing that forests have not yet lost in that country distinctive characteristics. In the vicinity of the Ural mountains the birches, larches, and cedars, have ceased to form distinct forests, but are associated with other kinds of trees: with firs on marshy grounds ; with pines on stony places.

In the *Izvestia* of the Russian Geographical Society, issued towards the end of 1881, there appeared a paper by M. Olshevsky, from which it appeared that, comparing surveys which were made in the province of Ufa before 1841 with the distribution of forests which had then been recently reported, the area of forests which at the previous time was about 17,577,000 acres had then been reduced by at least 3,500,000 acres, although the population was very sparse—less than three souls per square mile—and had been still less some time before.

In the forest lands attached to the copper-smelting works belonging to Colonel V. A. Pashkoff, at Bogo-yavlensk, and at Verchotov, both in the district of Sterlinatamak, in the Government of Ufa, which were visited by my friend, the method of exploitation followed is similar in many respects to that known in France as *Furetage*. Of this method of exploitation I have given in a volume entitled *Introduction to the Study of Modern Forest Economy** the following account :—

Furetage is a method of exploiting coppice woods composed of trees which reproduce shoots from the stump freely, and can reproduce a wood or forest without the aid of self-sown seed. It may be considered a modification of *Jardinage* applicable to the exploitation of such trees, though not to others; and the designation given to it in contradistinction to *Jardinage* has been given from some fancied resemblance to that of a ferret ferreting out what it is in pursuit of, as the other designation has been given in reference to some fancied resemblance to that of the kitchen gardener in gathering his crops. But in practice it is assimilated to *La Methode à tire et aire*.

'*Furetage*,' says the late Professor Bagneris, Inspector of Forests, and Professor at the Forest School of Nancy, in a work entitled *Elements of Sylviculture*,† ' consists in cutting the strongest shoots out of a clump, and in leaving the weaker ones. The wood-cutter returns to the same place every eight or ten years, and if the poles are cut at the

---

* *Introduction to the Study of Modern Forest Economy.*—In this there are brought under consideration the extensive destruction of forests which has taken place in Europe and elsewhere, with notices of disastrous consequences which have followed—diminished supply of timber and firewood, droughts, floods, landslips, and sand-drifts—and notices of the appliances of Modern Forest Science successfully to counteract these evils by conservation, planting, and improved exploitation, under scientific administration and management.

† *Elements of Sylviculture : a Short Treatise on the Scientific Cultivation of the Oak and other Hardwood Trees.* Translated from the French by E. E. Fernandez and A. Smythies, B.A., Indian Forest Service. London : William Rider & Son ; Simpkin, Marshall, & Co. 1882.

age of twenty-four or thirty years —(*i.e.*, if the rotation is of twenty-four or thirty years)—the clumps are composed of shoots of three different ages.' It is a method of exploitation applied chiefly to beech coppice wood.

The beech is a tree which is not well adapted for exploitation as coppice, but it can be exploited thus advantageously. There are in France about 100,000 acres of beech coppice, belonging for the most part to private proprietors. These are situated chiefly in that part of France formerly known as Morvan, on the Swiss side of the Jura, and at the foot to the Pyrenees; and there they are frequently subjected to this mode of exploitation.

An exhaustive article on the *Furetage* of the beech in the Pyrenees, by M. E. Guinier, may be found in the *Revue des Eaux et Forets* for 1883 (pp. 469-477, 527-541). His object is to show how an improved modification of this method of exploitation may remedy several evils, and secure several advantages, in coppice woods, which are thus treated; and in pursuit of this object he addresses himself chiefly to the objections of those who are so satisfied with it that they are unwilling to make any change. After discussing at considerable length much which is involved in the failures which have followed this method of exploitation, M. Guinier passes under review objections which have been taken to any attempt to improve it, and answers these *seriatim*. The objections thus treated are the following :—

It is said (1) *Furetage* is excellent inasmuch as it ensures the conservation of coppice woods; this has been established by experience : why seek for anything other than it is ?

2. What is defective in *Furetage* lies not in the method, but in the practice and application made of this; and we ought not to hold the method responsible for abuses which have crept into it in practice.

3. *Furetage* comprises a collection of harmonious rules

which have for their object to protect the interests of the regeneration of beech copse woods, which is a complex and delicate task ; it is impossible to condense these rules into a formula—simple, brief, and precise, which may be applicable without peril to innumerable cases in practice. It is, moreover, sufficient that the agents who have to manage beech copsewoods should know the end they have to keep before them ; it is then for them, from the resources supplied by their preparation and experience, to find out the means of accomplishing this applicable to the circumstances of each case.

4. It should be borne in mind that treatment as a timber forest is that alone which properly suits the beech, and even the partisans of *Furetage* can scarcely consider this method of exploitation as other than provisional, and one which ought only to be applied pending the transformation of the coppice wood into a timber forest, which should be the end of all foresters. What good, then, can be expected from seeking at great trouble to modify the existing order of things ?

Having replied to these several objections, M. Guinier states what he has to recommend, premising, however, that inasmuch as it admits the reservation of *balliveaux*, or seed-bearing standards, it is questionable whether the designation *Furetage* would still be applicable. And he expresses a kind of preference for another designation ; he says :—' I believe we must surrender the name. As a matter of fact, the principle of *Furetage* is the removal of the shoots which are in a dominant state and the constitution of a reserve taken, except occasionally, from the dominated shoots. And if we in principle prescribe the constitution of a reserve, more or less abundant, chosen from the dominating productions, we resume the principle of *Taillis sous futaie*—copse as the under-growth of a timber forest ; and whatever may be the proportions of the two constituents, a felling must present the aspect of one adapted to that mode of growth.'

D

In his treatise M. Guinier remarks that in view of the
principle underlying this method of exploitation it seems
to be a most certain and most simple mode of exploitation;
but in practice it is not found to be so.   He alleges that
from the first there do not exist the three well defined
divisions of shoots.   He adds that in the mountains where
vegetation is slow the shoots of thirty years cannot be
distinguished from those of twenty years growth when,
by any means whatsoever, the full development of the
former has been impeded.   The shoots of different divisions often preponderate in some one or more positions
instead of being dispersed equally among the others; and
the removal of them occasions an unequal exposure of the
soil, and of the younger shoots, which is contrary to the
very spirit of *Furetage;* and further, from whatever cause
it comes about, there is a very great diversity in the cubic
measurement of the produce from exploitation in this
method, which has given occasion for incessant modifications, and temporary suspensions of it, and for discussions.   From all which many many have arrived at the
conclusion borne out by facts that it is a method of
exploitation which is uncertain in its results and ill-
defined.

In the Pyrenees the formulas laid down for direction
are very variable, and various. In some cases two periods
of exploitation are established, in other cases three; and
the prescriptions vary much with time and place.
According to some, it is required to cut all shoots of a
prescribed girth, and leave all others; and the measurement varies considerably.   According to another prescrip-
tion, all spreading shoots, all isolated shoots, all shoots
under a certain size, and all shoots bearing secondary
shoots of a certain size, should be reserved. But in the
application of the rule great diversities are observed. A
modification of this, determining more fully what shoots
are to be reserved, has been proposed, but again variations
occur in the practical application of this.   For a time it
was customary to reserve from amongst the most vigorous

growing trees from fifty to sixty standards on every hec-
tare, but this was abandoned on the ground that these
standards were virtually bastard timber trees; and by
some there has been advocated the reservation of a certain
number of veritable *balliveaux*, reserved trees to supply seed.

By Professor Bagneris in his *Manuel de Sylviculture*, published in 1873, it is remarked that the coppice woods
treated thus were at that time little known, and had
perhaps not been sufficiently studied. Thus may the
diversities mentioned be accounted for.

With the explanations cited M. Guinier proceeds to
state what reserves he would propose. These are :—

1. *Anciens ; Modernes ; Balliveaux de l'Age N.*, which
are designations given respectively to trees left after one
complete revolution of successive fellings ; trees left after
two of these ; and trees left after three or more ; and,

2. All underwood composed of spreading shoots or
bushy suckers, and of all shoots below a prescribed
measurement at a height of four inches.

Several explanations and illustrations of what is meant
are given ; and in regard to advantages to be secured, he
says :—' These are the following :—

' 1. Sufficient shelter; and this as complete as may be
required according to circumstances, is secured for the
stumps, by the reserving of underwood and *balliveaux ;*

' 2. The maintenance on the stumps (save with an
exception always restricted) of twigs belonging to the
underwood and the *balliveaux,* serving to keep up the flow
of sap ;

' 3. An advance of many years increase obtained by the
reserving of the underwood ;

' 4. The *embroussaillement* of felling proper to prevent
damage done by cattle, and resulting also from the reserving of the underwood.

' These are advantages which it is sought to secure by
the old method of *Furetage,* and they are common to both
methods ; the following, on the contrary, pertain exclu-

sively to the new method, which is designed to accomplish, under like conditions, that in which the former is
defective and calls for reform.

' 5. The production of timber of large dimensions (if the
ground be suitable) which may be employed in industrial
operations.

' 6. The enrichment of the standing wood material
and the progressive augmentation of the production;

' 7. The production of natural sowings by means of the
seed cast abundantly by the reserves; and the amelioration of the crop by the aid of natural reproduction;

' 8. Preparation for a state of timber forest, by facilita-
ting the management required for proceeding promptly to
the transformation when the moment for this shall have
come;

' 9. The application of treatment the most advantageous
under every point of view, to the beech coppice which
cannot be converted into timber forest, be it on account of
economical considerations, or be it on account of the
poverty of the land.

' Let us compare now the spirit of the method proposed
with that of the old system of *Furetage*, and cast a glance
at the general results of the two methods of procedure.

' One can establish easily two essential differences.

' In the old *Furetage* each shoot was considered individually; and the necessary precautions were taken to
secure the life of the stump, and the prosperous growth of
the shoots to be obtained.   Further, the shoots in a
dominant condition were exploited, and the dominated
shoots were reserved awaiting the attainment by these
of a maximum of dimensions which was variable.

' On the contrary, by the employment of the proposed
formula :

' 1. The consideration of each shoot separately is abandoned in favour of the consideration of the prosperity of
the crop in a mass.   This method of looking at the subject is conformable to the modern and generally adopted
method of attending to the culture of woods, the prescrip-

tions of which relate to forest masses, and not to the trees individually. It is thus in the manœuvring of a *corps d'armée*, or of a battalion, or of even a platoon of soldiers, the individuality of the soldier is effaced. Attention to be given to the development of each subject pertains to arboriculture, whilst it is the development of the forest mass which is what pertains to sylviculture; no doubt the forest mass is composed of trees, as the army is composed of soldiers, and it is no more possible to lay down strictly rules of sylviculture without taking into account the requirements of the tree, than it is to determine the manœuvres of an army without having regard to the constitution of the soldier, to his strength, and to the maintenance of his health. But it seems as unreasonable to try to maintain any exploitation whatever without risking the loss of some shoots, or of some trees, the maintenance of which might be useful, as it would be strange for a warrior to hesitate to lead a battalion under fire, through fear that some men may be struck by the enemy's projectiles. In our fellings under this modification of coppice wood growing in a timber forest, what imports it that some stumps here and there may die? They will be replaced ten times, and a hundred times, more abundantly by the natural sowings.

' 2. The exploitation does not relate any longer to shoots in the dominant state, as in *Furetage;* and it does not relate to shoots in the dominated condition alone, as in ordinary coppice woods under timber; it relates actually mainly to what is in the intermediate condition, and each exploitation removes first what is in this intermediate state, and then a portion only of what is in the dominant state, consisting of abandoned reserves.

' Is it further required to give the means of comparing this modified *Furetage* with the old *Furetage?*

' It is clear that the first-mentioned method stands to the second as *Taillis sous futaie,* coppice under timber, does in relation to simple coppice; but the difference, it seems, is more accentuated, as in simple coppice there are still reserved *balliveaux*, or standards selected from amongst the strongest shoots.'

M. Guinier discusses the matter in all its details ; and he states at what places in France *Furetage* is practised, and the extent to which it is there carried out. But upon these discussions and statements I do not feel called upon to enter. In *Introduction to the Study of Modern Forest Economy* there is given information in regard to *Taillis sous futaie*.

In regard to *Furetage*, Professor Bagneris writes in his work which I have cited :—' It does not appear to us that this method of exploitation should be generally adopted, because, in the first place, it seems preferable to grow the beech as a timber forest,—and for private proprietors, who possess forests of this tree, as coppice with seed-yielding standards. If the standards are cut early enough, they will not injure the underwood they overtop, especially if the rotation is sufficiently long, and they will shed seed by which the growing stock will be kept full. Moreover, although *Furetage* has hitherto preserved beech coppices in a more or less satisfactory condition, it presents many disadvantages. Thus it is exceedingly difficult to cut a certain number of shoots in a clump without injuring the rest ; and in any case the labour is more costly. Besides this, cutting up the wood is not so easy when the shoots left standing are to be preserved from injury ; and it is necessary either to remove the former on men's backs, or to allow carts to come in among the standing crops—a proceeding which is necessarily productive of damage.'

M. Guinier may allege that he has devised a method of securing the good without the evil. And there is a modification of *Furetage** similar to what he advocates being carried out here advantageously.

---

* Oftener than once exception has been taken to my making use of such terms as *Furetage ;* but I am helpless in the matter. One writer, whom I highly esteem, remarks :—' It is to be regretted, we think, that Dr Brown should not have found some English equivalents for the French terms he employs. Surely " replanting or planting"

In the forests of Colonel Pashkoff at Bogoyavlensk and at Verchotov, the method of exploitation is essentially this of *Furetage*, but with certain modifications suggested by the proprietor. The following is a summary of information procured for me by my friend from the foresters in charge :—

'In the former there are 57,559 desiatins, or 155,400 acres, of which 43,037 desiatins are forests; in the latter nearly 47,073 desiatins, or 127,100 acres, of which 32,055 desiatins are forests.

'In the former the trees are oak, Norway maple, elm, aspen, lime, birch, and a proportionally small number of pine.

'In the latter the broad-leaved trees are of the same kinds, but there are about 7000 desiatins of fir and pine. In the former there are still about 9000 desiatins of virgin forest ; the remainder consists of trees ranging from one to fifty years old. In the latter there are about 7000 desiatins of virgin forest, and the remainder consists of trees varying from one to sixty years of age.

'In the former there is felled annually a section of about 200 desiatins, the oak trees alone being left standing, and this produces about 2000 square fathoms of a prescribed thickness, which is converted into charcoal ; in the latter the sections of forest felled annually are about 250 desiatins in extent. In these also the oaks are reserved, and the produce is about 2,500 fathoms, which in like manner is made into charcoal.

'The sections devoted to exploration are in both forty in number. In the cleared sections the trees grow up more densely than before, and by the expiry of the forty years cycle they are again fit for being felled.

---

is to the full as expressive as *réboisement*, " management" as intelligible as *exploitation*, " clearance " as *sartage*, " selection" as *jardinage*, " rotation " or " cropping" for *la methcde à tire et aire*, " coppice " for *furetage* and *taillis sous futaie*.' But it is the case that none of the English terms suggested is the equivalent of the French term for which it is suggested that it might be substituted ; and, unhappily, I do not know any which is so in the present stage of forest science in Britain. I have sought to secure precision by the course I have followed here and in other passages open to the same objection, deeming this of importance in existing circumstances.

'In neither is any growing or felled wood disposed of for firewood, but dead or fallen trees are disposed of to the inhabitants of the locality as fuel at a fixed charge of 1.30 rouble per chimney per annum.

'No trees are sold for timber or transport. The trees of the young and cleared ground are about double in number that of the virgin forest, but it is more pecuniarily remunerative to keep the land under cereal crops or hay than under forest trees.

'In the first-mentioned forest land there are employed 23 forest watchmen, with salaries varying from 8 to 20 roubles per month; in the other forest lands, 16 forest watchmen are employed at wages varying from 4 to 12 roubles per month : the rouble is at present equal to 2s., but its equivalent in sterling money varies with the rate of exchange, it has been 2s. 6d., and in a normal state of the exchange it is supposed to be equal to 3s.'

CHAPTER III.

MISHAPS AND DIFFICULTIES ENCOUNTERED IN TRAVELLING IN EASTERN RUSSIA.

As an inducement to me to accompany my friends on their visit to Ufa, it was jestingly proposed that we should not only visit the forests of Bogoyovensk and Vergator, but that some of us should proceed to Orenburg, in the extreme south of the Government; and thence advance beyond the boundary, and see something of Siberia. The proposal was in jest; but the idea having been once suggested it was deemed feasible; and some of the party set out to carry it into execution. To the journey a brief reference was made in the preceding chapter. Of what was experienced in making the attempt to reach Orenburg my friend wrote to me :—

'To resume my narrative, which, please notice, is not founded on any journal report, but altogether on memory : Interesting as everything was, villages with their various tribes (each village being distinct)—first, it may be a Bashkir or a Tartar one, then a Russian, followed by a Tchuvash one (Mordins and other tribes were spoken of, but none were distinctly pointed out), the road was often traceable for miles by a straight line of trees; the hills ran parallel with us on our left, many of them were of fine shape, but, with a few exceptions, bare of trees ; then gradually hills appeared on our right, and we were soon closed in by darkness as well as hills. The morning found us at a station named Uralsk. We had been during the night crossing a spur of the Ural range running at right angles to the main range. The heights cannot be great; but I cannot speak from observation, for both going and returning we slept most of the time, the night not

allowing any extended vision as far as our immediate
surroundings were concerned, but giving a view of the
starry heavens such as an astronomer would delight in if
not encumbered by the *embarras de richesses*. Our course
during the day and night was almost due south, from, if
I remember correctly, 37° to about 32°, in longitude about
74₀. At Uralsk I made a mistake which has cost me
dear. Awakened out of sleep, while horses were being
changed, I preferred a walk (as I had done several times
the previous day) to breakfast, thinking that could be
obtained at next station. I got my walk, and even a nice
refreshing wash in a river just outside the village, but lost
all chance of food till we should reach our destination.
We soon entered the steppes, a series of swelling downs
well cultivated,—in fact the first part of the journey was
through a populous district, one or two villages being
generally within view, though not on our line of march.
After crossing the river Salmish we came to the mining
district, which I may note is being brought more and
more into cultivation—wheat being more profitable than
the small percentage of copper yielded by the mine. Not a
tree was visible for miles, though I should say my range of
vision was limited much by the natural conformation of the
grounds, as I do not remember anywhere seeing a plain,
but always a series of hills of no great height, and with a
long incline. The long rolling waves of the Pacific or
Atlantic, if suddenly solidified, would present the same
appearance.

'Here my narrative must close. That day sixty versts
under a broiling sun, without food till 3 P.M., was more
than my poor frame could stand. Fever set in, and a
bilious attack, which made the visit to Orenburg impossible, or any inspection of the mines, or search for fossils,
on which I had reckoned so much. After four days I was
placed in the conveyance for return, but to break the
journey at Verchotov, the other copper mine of Mr Pashkoff. Here I first learned the secret of comfort in tarantass travelling. My brother-in-law, who accompanied me,

has a special talent for arranging the hay, &c., and, weak as I was, I passed comfortably through the night, and even bathed in a river the next morning. Then came five or six hours of a dreadful journey—tropical sun, bad horses, rough road—so that I reached my destination almost fainting, and needing to be physicked and nursed.

' How I have missed a better knowledge of botany and geology during this trip! and regretted having no books of reference with me, or knowing how to preserve plants! Several plants took my attention as not seen by me before. The first I plucked in Kazan, but subsequently found abounding everywhere in the Ufa and Orenburg Governments, was a blue flower. A stiff stalk, about a foot in height, with a series of buds arranged spirally, I think, from root to top. One bud, rarely two, opened into a simple flower, about an inch in diameter, composed of a single row of petals. In some cases the opened flower was near the ground, but mostly half-way up the stem or near its top.

' Another plant was a small spear thistle, the head sometimes, but more frequently the whole plant, of a bright pale blue colour. This I found often, generally on hill sides, and it had a most peculiar appearance, accustomed as we are to see colours, beside green, limited to the petals.

' Of another plant I plucked one specimen some distance up a hill-side, but I saw more afterwards when driving through a wood. I think you would class it among reeds or rushes—a circular stem full of sap—leaves, I forget, but think, rather long, the stem ending in a head of bloom, blood red, almost circular, composed of many separate flowers, arranged much like the thistle-down, but having no affinity to it.

' In driving through one of the woods I saw a plant very much resembling the garden phlox, but could not get out to examine it more closely. The report of bears being in the vicinity, and the fear of snakes in the long grass, made me too cowardly.

'On the banks of the Bielaya, which I had to cross many times in various places, I found the wild hop growing luxuriantly. Under cultivation the district yields wheat, millet, buckwheat, hemp, oats, with a little flax and some rye.'

Again and again I have heard like complaints to those of my friend in regard to the discomforts of travelling by tarantass, where this has not been properly packed with the *impedimenta* with which most travellers on a long journey find it necessary to encumber themselves.
The conveyance is composed of a body ranging in form from that of half a large cask cut longitudinally to that of an old worn-out phaeton, being distinguished from a *telega* by having a hood and apron, and four wheels, upon the axles of which it is supported by two long poles or young trees, possessed of considerable elasticity.
In a companion volume, entitled *Forest Lands and Forestry of Northern Russia*,* I had occasion to cite the experience of Hepworth Dixon in travelling through the forests in the Government of Archangel, in which he says:—' Our only change is in the track itself, which passes from sand drifts to slimy beds, from grassy fields to rolling logs. In a thousand versts we count a hundred versts of log-road, two hundred versts of sand, three hundred versts of grass, four hundred versts of waterway and marsh.
'If the sands are bad the logs are worse. One night we spend in a kind of protest, dreaming that our luggage has been badly packed, and that on daylight coming it shall be laid in some easier way. The trunk calls loudly for a

---

* *Forest Lands and Forestry of Northern Russia.* Details are given of a trip from St. Petersburg to the forests around Petrozavodsk on Lake Onega, in the Government of Olonetz ; a description of the forests in that government by Mr Judrae, a forest official of high position, and of the forests of Archangel by Mr Hepworth Dixon, of Lapland, of the Land of the Samoides and of Nova Zembla ; of the exploitation of the forests by *Jardinage*, and of the evils of such exploitation ; and of the export timber trade, and disposal of forest products. In connection with discussions of the physical geography of the region information is supplied in regard to the contour and general appearance of the country ; its flora, its forests, and the palæontological botany of the regions beyond, as viewed by Professor Heer and Count Saporta ; its fauna, with notices of game, and with copious lists of coleoptera and lepidoptera, by Forst-Meister Guenther, of Petrozavodsk.

change. My seat by day, my bed by night, this box has a leading part in our little play; but no adjustment of the other traps, no stuffing in of hay and straw, no coaxing of the furs and skins, suffice to appease the fitful spirit of that trunk. It slips and jerks beneath me, rising in pain at every plunge. Coaxing it with skins is useless; soothing it with wisps of straw is vain. We tie it with bands and belts; but nothing will induce it to lie down. How can we blame it? Trunks have rights as well as men; they claim a proper place to lie in; and my poor box has just been tossed into this tarantass, and told to lie quiet on logs and stones.

'Still more fitful than this trunk are the lumber verte-bræ in my spine. They hate this jolting day and night; they have been jerked out of their sockets, pounded into dust, and churned into curds. But then these mutineers are under more control than the trunk; and when they begin to murmur seriously, I still them in a moment by hints of taking them a drive through Bitter Creek.'

In regard to the packing of luggage in a tarantass, Dr Lansdell, in his volume entitled *Through Siberia*, tells:—

'The packing of the vehicle requires nothing short of a Siberian education. Avoid boxes as you would the plague! The edges and corners will cruelly bruise your back and legs. Choose rather flat portmanteaus and soft bags, and spread them on a layer of hay at the bottom of the tarantass. Then put over them a thin mattress, and next a hearth-rug. When we entered Tiumen, women besieged us with these hearth-rugs, as I thought them. Not knowing what they were for, I could not conceive what they meant by such conduct. Had my companion been a lady, I should have deemed that they thought us on a bridal trip, and about to set up housekeeping. But I was innocent of all such devices, and chased the women away. When it was discovered what the carpets were for, I regretted not having bought one. Next, put at the back of the carriage two or more pillows of the softest down, for which please send on your order in advance, because these must be bought as opportunity offers. If a housewife has finished the manufacture of a down pillow she wishes to sell, she will bring it into Ekaterineburg to market, but if you want such a thing on a given day, you may search the town and not get one.

'You may now get in, cover your legs with a rug, and watch them harness the horses. Siberian post-horses are sorry objects to look at, but splendid creatures to go. A curry-comb probably never touches their coats; but, under the combined influence of coaxing, scolding, screaming, and whip, they attain a pace which in England would be adjudged as nothing short of " furious driving." They are smaller than English horses, but much hardier, and are driven two, three, four, or even five or more, abreast. The Russian harness is a complicated affair, the most noticeable feature being the *douga*, 'or arched bow, over the horse's neck. To the foreigner this looks a needless incumbrance, but the Russian declares that it holds the whole concern together. The rods are fastened to the ends of the bow, and the horse's collar in turn to the shafts, so that the collar remains a fixture, against which the horse is obliged to push. The shafts are supported by a saddle and pad on the back, and do not touch the horse's body. The centre horse only is in rods; those on either side, how many soever they be, are called a "pair," and are merely attached by ropes. If you have been wise, you have bought at the *Gostinnoi Dvor* about 20 yards of inch rope to go all round the back of the vehicle, and to which are attached the two outer horses. The post-men are supposed to supply such a rope, but theirs are often thin and rotten. It is well, too, to take several fathoms of half-inch rope. One of the wheels may become rickety, and threaten to fall to pieces, in which case the rope will be needed to interlace the spokes. A third supply should be laid in of still smaller cord, in case of spraining a pole or the rods. Do not forget to purchase besides a hatchet. All these we took, and more than all were wanted.

'When the driver, or *yemstchik*, has taken his seat, the horses will not stay a minute. Indeed, in some districts, the horses' heads are held while the driver mounts, and, when freed, they start with a bound. And now begin your pains and penalties !

'When at Nijni Tagilsk, we descended by ladders 600 feet into a copper-mine, and came up in the same manner, we were warned that on the following day we should be terribly stiff; but I aver that the consequences were as nothing compared with those of the first day's travelling by tarantass. The roughness of the roads and the lack of springs combine to cause a shaking up, the very remembrance of which is painful. Let the reader imagine himself about to descend a hill at the foot of which is a stream crossed by a corduroy bridge of poles. The ordinary tarantass has no brake, the two outer horses are in loose harness, and the one in rods has no breeching. The whole weight of the machine, therefore, is thrown on his collar, and the first half of the hill is descended as slowly as may be. But the speed soon increases, first because the rod-horse cannot help it, and next because an impetus is desired to carry you up the opposite hill. All three horses, therefore, begin to pull, and, long before the bridge is reached, you are going at a flying pace, and everybody has to "hold on." The bridge is approached; and now comes the excruciating moment. Most likely— almost to a certainty—the rain has washed away the earth a good six inches below the first timber of the bridge, against which bump! go your fore-wheels, and thump! go your hind ones; whilst fare and driver are alike shot up high into the air. I have a lively recollection of these ascents, some of which were so high that, when travelling from Archangel to Lake Onega, we had the hood removed, lest our skulls should strike the top. Happily, all roads are not so perilously rough, and, briefly to summarise my experience of them, I should say that

that those of Tobolsk and Tomsk are muddy, causing the
yemstchiks, when possible, to avoid them—to go into
lanes and by-ways, over hillocks and fallen timber, and
down into holes and ditches, all of which give variety to
the route.   The Yeneseisk roads deserve nothing but
praise; they are well kept, and would be reckoned good
in England.   The Irkutsk ways deteriorate, and those
beyond Baikal are worse than all; for the Buriat yemstchiks drive you furiously over hillocks, rocks, and stones.

'Nor are roads the only things to be traversed; there
are numerous streams and rivers—some with bridges, but
more without. Through some of these your horses simply
walk; on others there is a well-kept ferry, upon which
you and your carriage are drawn or rowed. On one
occasion our vehicle was put on the ferry, and the horses
made to swim the stream. It sometimes happens, however, especially in early spring, that the ice or floods have
carried away or damaged the ferry, and a flat-bottomed
boat is temporarily substituted.   In this manner we
crossed the Tom. The tarantass was lifted by degrees
into the boat, one wheel at a time. The boat was only
just wide enough to take the vehicle, and we were advised
to let down the hood, lest the wind should blow us over.
This was about the only time I felt nervous, and I confess
being thankful when we safely reached the opposite
shore.

'The cost of these pleasures of travel is not so great in
Siberia as might be supposed. In the western division,
where pasture is abundant, the hire of each horse is only
about a halfpenny per mile. In Eastern Siberia, the fare
is exactly double. Horses are changed about every ten or
fifteen miles, and each new driver looks for a gratuity,
euphemistically called " money for *tea*." On the amount of
the " tip" depends your speed. Ten kopecks are often
given, but we found fifteen put the boys in better humour,
and we made from a 100 to 130 miles a day. Two hundred
versts in a day and night, for summer travelling, is considered good, and we sometimes did it; but given a Rus-

sian merchant, bound for a fair where his early arrival will give him command of the market, and then a "tip" of say a rouble a stage, will in winter get him over 300 versts, or 200 miles a day. It is common to hear Siberians boast of quick journeys made thus, but they are usually attained only at cruel cost to the horses. The reader may judge what speed can be made from a story told us at Tieumen of a Governor-General of Eastern Siberia, whom the late Emperor, some twelve winters ago, required on an emergency at Petersburg, a distance from Irkutsk of 3,700 miles. The General was put in a bear's skin, wrapped up like a bundle, placed in a sledge, and in eleven days was brought to the capital. Several horses dropped dead on the way, an ear was cut from each as a voucher, and the journey continued. When governors of provinces travel, they are supplied with the best horses in the villages, and sometimes have them changed at the half stage, so as to spare the animals whilst securing extra speed.

' Having said this much about the vehicles, horses, and roads, the reader may wonder how it fares with the traveller in the matters of lodging and board, which brings me to the subject of post-houses. These, like the post-horses, are the property of the Government, and are of very varied quality, from the best—which have all the appearance and the comfort of a roomy, well-established English farm-house or country inn—to the worst, which are little better than hovels. Certain features, however, are common to them all. On one side of the door, as you enter, will be found the room in which the post-folks and their children live, and on the other will be one or more rooms reserved for travelling guests. The guests' room will never contain less than the following articles : a table, a chair, a candlestick, a bed, or rather a bench—padded, if in a good house, but of bare boards in the humbler ones —an *ikon* or sacred picture, a looking-glass, and sundry framed notices. One of these notices is a tariff of meat and drink—not that you are to suppose for a moment that any amount of money would purchase the luxuries

E

'Their provisions are plentiful and good, and their tariff
of charges is moderate. On the whole, a very pleasant
week may be spent by an observant man on this river
journey. The few towns passed on the way break the
monotony of the voyage, and the scenery is not without
its peculiar recommendations; though I cannot endorse
the opinion of the travellers who say that the river Kama,
which we enter a short distance below Kazan, is splendid.
Such eulogists must measure their admiration by a lower
standard of beauty than do I.

'Beyond Perm the journey is easy enough to any part
of Siberia; it is certainly a little tedious, but even that
depends in a great measure on a man's own resources for
amusement, because there is plenty of pretty scenery, hill,
wood, and water, which are a delightful compensation for
a little jolting about, especially to a traveller from that
flatter part of Russia, where even as much as a mole-hill
upon the horizon is a natural curiosity, and the wearied
eye looks round in vain for a relief to the everlasting
monotony of the interminable sandy or grass-grown
steppe.

'The finest town I have seen in Siberia is Ekaterineburg, the frontier town between European and Asiatic
Russia, a position which gives it many advantages. Irkutsk is also a nice town; but Ekaterineburg has the
superiority in several respects. It contains a population
of 25,000 souls, and is handsomely built, possessing several
fine churches, and a great number of brick and stone
houses; among which some deserve to be called rather
palaces, also a mint and large mechanical works belonging
to the Government. It has also a theatre, a club, and two
really good hotels; and, on the whole, is as unlike a city
on the outside borders of civilisation, and in the close
neighbourhood of Asiatic barbarism, as it is possible to
imagine. I am sure that, when eating the *dinêr à la carte*,
supplied by M. Plotnikoff, at the best hotel, I found myself
as closely surrounded by the externals of civilisation as I
could be in any European city.

'There is plenty of refined society to be met with in all Siberian towns, and the time of one's sojourn there always glides away pleasantly, the regularity and evenness of the climate being an addition to the enjoyment of life.'

All my informants agree in giving what many would deem fabulous accounts of the comforts and luxuries to be enjoyed in Ekaterineburg. Did time and occasion serve I might enlarge upon these till the most jovial amongst us would be ready to say,—I wish I were there! Of the natural scenery Barry writes:—'The woods in the summer are beautiful; although the long days are hot, the evenings are always cool and rather damp; and the wild flowers grow everywhere in great luxuriance. Strawberries and raspberries, currants, cherries, and many other kinds of wild edible berries are gathered from the woods in great quantities, and sent off to supply the markets of neighbouring towns, which receive all their fruits from these wild growths.'

Speaking of the resources of the country, he says: 'There are gold, silver, copper, lead, iron, coal, and salt, and dense forests still undisturbed. I have travelled over miles of mineral wealth, for day after day, through interminable woods. I have looked from the highest mountains, and from horizon to horizon, and seen nothing but thickly-timbered forests covering the hills and valleys. All this is yet to be utilised. There it stands, idle, as abundant as man can want, and only waiting for the axe of the immigrant, when the tide of colonisation shall set towards Siberia, under the auspices of the liberal policy recently inaugurated by the Russian Government. . .

'The resources of Siberia are immense. Few people have any idea of their importance. Her mineral wealth is almost unexplored; in the few places where it is worked it is so most unsatisfactorily, and under the worst possible management. To judge of the importance of this part of the wealth of Russia, consider only the Ural mountains, which extend from north to south a distance of 1,200 miles, and

their slopes are known to contain more or less gold along
the whole extent of them. Yet they are only worked in
a few places, and there not as they ought to be. Consider,
again, the large tract of copper-producing country, and
how few are the works scattered here and there upon it.
And so it is with iron and all other minerals—they are
all comparatively neglected.' And he goes on to say :—

    ' Whenever I travel about Siberia I always think, why
is it that our countrymen are sent all the way to the
antipodes in search of a colony? I speak of those who set
out with a small capital. Here, nearer home, they can get
better land cheaper than in many of our colonies; they
can live more cheaply, can hire labour cheaply, and enjoy
many advantages of civilisation which they would want in
the colonies. Not only does farming here, but all other
industrial enterprises likewise, offer a good occupation and
the promise of a fortune to a man who courageously and
judiciously inaugurates and carries them through. In
short, I can think of no other country in the world which
offers the same advantages to a young man with a small
capital as Siberia.' And he gives illustrations of successful
enterprise by self-made men, who were born serfs.

    My late friend Mr Wilkinson, of whom I have already
spoken, an intelligent engineer, who had travelled extensively in Russia and Siberia, residing for a time in different
places whither he was called by his professional duties—in
compliance with a wish which I expressed for some idea
of the general aspect of this region, wrote to me :—' I will
not weary you with dry details of the mineral and vegetable productions which are to be found in the Ural region.
Suffice it to say that, in a circuit of some 3000 miles, you
find every variety of tree indigenous to the temperate
zone.
    ' If you wish to see a country, you must travel through
it by horses on the cross roads, not by rail, nor on the
open beaten track ; and in passing over those gradually
sloping mountains of Kushvinsky, Neviansk, Polieffskoi,

Oafalei, Nazo-Petroffsky, Urzan, Zalatanst, Miask, and others, I have often been enchanted and charmed with the variegated landscape, and the picturesqueness of the scene. Trees of every foliage, flowers of every hue, mosses, ferns, and grasses of exquisite form, are there. And when you get to the top of a hill a grand amphitheatre stretches out before you, unfolding a magnificent panorama, embracing many hundreds of square versts in one view, of river and lake, forest and plain, flocks and cultivated fields. Every bush and every tree resounds with the delicious warble of thousands of inimitable rivals of Patti—linnet, nightingale, starling, and thrush; and perhaps the beauty of the picture is enhanced by a peaceful town or a busy zavod in the distance, with their prettily painted roofs, gilded domes, and glittering spires.

'Often have I stopped and tried to drink in the sublimity of those scenes, and, in the words of the poet, I have exclaimed, "Can imagination, with all its boast, paint scenes like these!" Then I have often gotten out of my conveyance and collected specimens unknown to me, and called to mind the words of Him who understood nature's book the best, "I say unto you that even Solomon in all his glory was not arrayed like one of these." Then I have wondered where could be the brains of men contemplating such a sweet and beauteous view as this, having tongues in trees, books in the running brooks, sermons in stones, and yet trying to trace it all to spontaneous development. Of course it has been developed and brought to such beauty and perfection as we see it now; but who developed it? And the answer came to me in the words of Milton's immortal hymn :—

> "These are thy glorious works, Parent of good !
> Almighty ! Thine this universal frame !
> Thus wondrous fair ! thyself how wondrous then,
> Unspeakable, who sit'st above the heavens,
> To us invisible, or dimly seen
> In these, thy lowest works ! Yet these declare
> Thy goodness beyond thought, and power divine !"

'Speaking about sermons in stones, you find in parts of the Ural boulder stones of 200,000 and 300,000 pounds weight, some embedded in the earth, some lying on the surface, some piled one on another. How did they get there? How have such vast masses been moved? How have they been worn so round, and polished so smooth, at 3000 and 5000 feet above the present level of the sea?'

A little sketch was given to me by him incidentally of cultivated ground, which is in keeping with the preceding reference to the natural scenery of the region. If my readers will glance at it, I believe it will gratify them; but it is associated with incidents in the life of one of our countrymen who made it what it is, and notices of him suggest notices of others likewise engaged in engineering operations there, all of them to me so full of interest that unless I hold a firm rein I may be carried further from the forests than may seem to be consistent with our professed aim, though it would be difficult to say why a forester or a student of forest science should not enjoy a good story as fully as any other man. Let me premise that not a few of our countrymen have been employed in these works, occuping places of trust, with corresponding emolument. He wrote to me:—

'One day I received from my employer a note inviting me to take a drive with him and his friends, the Razanoffs, to a datch, or country house of their's, some fourteen versts out of Ekaterineburg. There were four of us. Each of my companions that day was a millionaire. I wonder if English millionaires would keep company with their servants. It was a delightful day, and a most picturesque drive on the main Siberian road to one of the most lovely scenes I ever put eyes upon. There were long and shady avenues of silver fir, weeping birch, fragrant spruce, flowering lime, graceful poplar, and that most beautiful of of all trees, the Siberian mountain ash. There was park and plain, lake and waterfall, gurgling fountains and crystal, teaming with aquatic plants and sportive fish.

Those rippling streams went meandering through green lawns, flowering shrubs, and mounds blazing with annuals. No mimic rockeries were required, such as I have seen even Chatsworth. Wild nature and graceful art combined altogether formed a picture that may be remembered, but cannot be drawn by words. There was a fine country seat on an eminence commanding the whole of this extensive and beautiful view. The adjacent peasants' shanties, the kitchen and garden, stables, out-houses, were all hidden from the house by trees, shrubs, and embankments, forming of themselves, an agreeable adjunct, all built in that pretty romantic old Boyrian style.

'While we were enjoying a sumptuous repast, provided for the occasion as Russians only can and will do these things, they related to me the history of the place.

'When Alexander I. was on the Ural, he found an Englishman, Mr Major, in charge of the mines at Parda, and so well pleased was he with him that he gave him more substantial proofs of his Imperial favour than orders or medals. He made him a deed of gift of this Crown estate, and Major had it converted into an earthly paradise. And just as he left it, I saw it. There was an Englishman's stamp, taste, and thoroughness about it everywhere. Fancy an English dirty mechanic in the beginning, in the long run rivalling an English lord! Allow me to relate an anecdote which they told me, characteristic of the man, and illustrative of that vien of humour with which the English are so embued that even transportation to Siberia cannot suppress it.

'One day Major received a notice that there was lying at the post-office a valuable parcel addressed to him. Away drives he himself next day in a carriage and pair, and when he gets it, home he comes as soon as he can. After impatiently unwrapping and unwrapping scores of foldings of beautiful fine tissue paper, he at last finds an old, dirty, worn-out *naumre*, or the cast-off bast-mat shoe of a mujik! He quietly pocketed the intended insult, and said nothing about it to any one; but he suspected

his man—a mining engineer, a cur of a fellow, who had
bothered him a good deal at the mines, and who was then
writhing under chagrin and envy at Major's prosperity.
He called in his old housekeeper. "Now," says he, "can
I confide in your faithfully carrying out a scheme I have
in my head ?" " Well, I have been with you so many years.
What do you mean?˙ what is it ?" " Well, upon pain of
instant dismissal, and deprivation of your expected pension
if you divulge my secret, I will tell you." "Agreed ; out
with it ! " " Very well. Take now this old shoe ; wash
it and clean it ; and then chop it up into very fine powder.
Let not a particle be lost." "And what then?" " You
shall learn that by and by. I am going to give a grand
dinner party, and intend to invite everybody, so you must
excel even yourself, especially in pies and puddings." The
Russians always rave about English roast-beef and plum-
puddings, and in keeping with this were these instructions
given. The dinner went off gloriously. Everybody was
delighted, but not a word had been spoken about the shoe
till towards the end of the feast, the suspected man called
out from the bottom of the table, "I say, Major, did you not
receive recently a valuable present? What was it? an
order ? or the conveyance of another estate as a further
reward for your past valuable services? It's not fair, you
know, to keep it from us ; you. ought ·to tell us." There
was a giggle, and a twitter went round, as evidently a good
many of the guests were cognisant of the trick, and they
were waiting for some fun at the expense of Major. But
they had reckoned without their host. For once the
Englishman was more than a match for them all ; and he
very quietly replied, " Before I answer your question, allow
me to ask of you, How did you like it?" "Why? how?
What do you mean, Mr Major?" " Well, you ought to
know best. You seem to have liked it ; and you have all
swallowed your fair share of it to-day, as my old cook,
after chopping it up into mince-meat, has mixed a portion
of your dirty old shoe in every pie, pudding, and sauce,
you have now eaten at my table ! "

'There was immediately a scene; some stormed, some vomited, especially the ladies, calling him a nasty, dirty, old pig. But most of the guests laughed heartily at the chop-fallen wag and would-be wit, by whom the shoe had been sent.

'Poor Major did not live long after this to enjoy the sweets of his repose. It turned out that there was a large quantity of gold on the estate; and the late Emperor Nicholas very nobly and generously reconfirmed his brother's gift, and left Major in undisturbed possession, with full liberty to wash the gold. But as it often happens what we think our greatest good proves our greatest evil. So was it now. Major very unwisely would persist in keeping his gold in his own cabinet, contrary to law, and despite the expostulations of his friends. The quantity at one time amounted to five poods, worth 100,000 roubles.

'One Sunday evening while he was reading his Bible in his bed-room, being about to retire to rest, he heard an unaccountable noise in the back passage, and after repeatedly calling out, "Tcho tam?" [Who's there?], and getting no answer, he took his bed-room candle and went to see what it was; but as he opened the door he was met by a blow on the head from an axe, which felled him to the ground to rise no more, while the murderous villians made of with their booty—the box of gold. It is a satisfaction to know that in a very ingenious way, which I have not time to describe, the deed was feretted out by a General specially appointed by the Emperor, and an admirer, and a friend of the Major. He re-covered the gold, sold off the estate to the present owners, the Razanoffs, then went to England and divided fairly a handsome fortune amongst all of the relatives of Major he could find. The actual perpetrator of the deed died under that dreadful infliction the gauntlet. The rest were sent to Siberia in irons for life. They had first killed a faithful old man and an equally faithful woman servant before they could get at Major. It is a somewhat remarkable coincidence that the Bible was found open at

the 12th chapter of St. Luke's gospel, where there are
such passages as these, " The ground of a certain rich man
brought forth abundantly ; " " What shall I do, because I
have no room where to bestow all my fruits and my goods ?"
and not improbably the murdered man had also read that
awful fiat, " This night shall thy soul be required of thee."
The open Bible may lead us to hope that his soul was
prepared to obey the dreadful summons, and that with
him it was sudden death, sudden glory. Major has left
behind him a high reputation on the Urals.'

   By the same friend I was supplied with much information in regard to countrymen of ours engaged in work
connected with the mines within the present century,
some of them having developed there into men almost
eccentric in their modes of life and relaxation. Notices
of them are not necessary to the accomplishment of my
design ; but looking upon them as I would upon peculi-
arities in the landscape, I feel as if they were part and
parcel of the scene I wish to bring before my readers. I
subjoin his notices of them here, leaving to my readers to
glance at them or not, as they may feel disposed. In continuation of his narrative, my friend wrote : —
   ' Allow me to relate one other anecdote of another
north countryman of ours, which is of a less melancholy
character than the last. Some time since there was employed
at the chief engineering establishment of all the Government Ural works at Ekaterineburg, an Englishman, a
Newcastle man, as head engineer, with a staff of Englishmen under him, who were first-class mechanics, well
known all over the Urals—smiths, model makers, fitters,
&c. He also had the good fortune to have a nice little
property presented to him, by the present Emperor ; and
he retired some time since with a nice little fortune of
about 60,000 roubles. This gentleman, as do many of his
countrymen, liked a good dinner, perhaps liking this before.
everything else. He also, like many others who enjoy
good luxury, was stout enough to have played Falstaff

without artificial stuffing. In the course of his duties he had to travel about from zavod to zavod; but he never did so without his lackey, his cook, and every accessory to his personal comfort, in a large, lumbering travelling carriage, drawn by four horses. It was so fitted up as to form a sleeping car by night, and then be folded up to form a little sitting room by day, the boot being well stocked with wines, provisions, and dainty snacks of every kind.

'Somewhere between Ekaterineburg and Allipieff, he stopped one night to take supper, after which his servants put him comfortably to bed in his conveyance. They then thought they would have a little jollification on their own account, and took the yemstchik or hired driver along with them. Just for a few moments had they got permission; but the minutes sped past, and they took no note of time; and as the " baron" was fast asleep he knew not how time was flying. At last the horses got impatient at being left out in the cold, and they set off quietly to trot home again. But after a little they had to descend a steep hill on the road, and as there was no one there to put on the brake to guide or to check them, the ponderous vehicle soon overpowered them, and began to rattle downwards at breakneck speed, threatening to smash everything to splinters. The extraordinary rocking, rumbling, and jolting of the monstrous carriage soon awoke poor Peter to a sense of his danger, and opening the window and yelling out to know the reason why, he found himself alone, with four runaway horses madly tearing along. Realising his position, and not knowing but that at any moment he might be either hurled into the ravine below or dashed against a tree on the upper side of the road cut out on the hill-side, he thought it would be better to choose a lesser evil, and throw himself out head foremost upon the road. The decision was soon made, and he took what he thought might be a leap for life, with no worse results than a good bruising and a rolling in the dust. But his troubles did not end here. He had no sooner sat down to recover himself from his fright than he was immediately covered with large stinging ants, mosquitoes, wasps, and gad-flies, which goaded him to madness. And in the very midst of his desperation, for he had begun to roll on the road as the best means of mitigating his agony, up drove a woman on horseback, going to the hay fields, for it was early dawn, and a fine summer's morning. But she, seeing the huge mountain of flesh rolling about on the road as does a porpoise in the sea, was about to gallop off back in alarm, thinking it something unearthly; when poor Peter, seeing her, cried " Stop, stop ! Matuska, Matuska, do stop ! and for any sake take pity upon me, and lend me your caftan to protect me from these poisonous beasts ! " Just as she had satisfied herself that it was a human being that was speaking to her, and was about to render him assistance, up came gasping the three men whose negligence had well nigh brought him to a still more disastrous end, and who had set off full speed as soon as they had discovered that horses and carriage and Barin had bolted. They did their best to rectify the evils their carelessness had brought about; they got back the carriage, for it arrived safe and sound at the station-house. They were profuse in their whining supplications for pardon, and in assurance that such a thing would never occur again; but this was all too little and too late to appease Peter. He returned home to give them a dose of the rod just to see, he said, whether they could endure stinging any better than he could. He could do that sort of thing then, and it is reported that he was very fond of doing it. He was a cold-blooded mortal, who never got into a passion, but never forgave a wrong or a mistake, fancied or real. He has left behind him a name on the Ural as much abhorred as Major's is adored.'

My friend goes on to say :—
· 'Had time permitted I should have liked to have said something about the habits and customs of the pure Russian merchant class up here, of the doings of the adminis-

trative officials, of the character and worship of the Nonconformists, Primitive Methodists, and the adherents to the
Solemn League and Covenant, for they all have their
representatives here, and very numerous they are. Also
of their method of making this beautiful and highly-
polished sheet iron of theirs; of the quality and condition
of the work-people at the zavods; of the tallow-boiling and
sheep-slaying business; of the mining corps of engineers;
of the imperial granite and marble works; of the lapi-
daries, the precious stone polishers, and engravers; of the
monastery in Ekaterineburg; of our own countrymen;
and of the towns, and society in general; but it is impossible to do justice here to all that relates to a district
so extensive and so interesting as is this.

'There are many other matters I should like to have
referred to had time permitted, especially what I have
seen of the exiles and convicts in Siberia, and my impressions and experience of my first travels among the semi-
barbarous tribes of the Chevash, Cheremish, Mondbee,
and others.

'You may perhaps think, and I feel it is the case, that
I have not drawn a very flattering portaiture of the
Russians, but that is only one side of the picture, the dark
side, and I can now give my view of the light side only in
a few words.

'The Russian, simple and uncontaminated by the
foreign adulteration, especially the landed gentry and the
inland population, have many a bright redeeming feature
that stands out in bold relief from that of the group I have
presented.

'Certainly they are to me an enigma. They seem to
unite the two extremes in every phase of their character:
Clean and filthy, orderly and slovenly, near and prodigal,
mean and ostentatious, educated and shallow, accomplished
and boorish, exact and indifferent, dogmatic and tolerant.
rigidly pious and lax of morals, early rising and sleeping
half the day. I sometimes think Voltaire's description of
the English will hit them off very well. Frothy at the

top, muddy at the bottom, good and clear in the middle.
And now, in conclusion, allow me to say that after fifteen
years' intimate acquaintance with them, of every class, I
unhesitatingly affirm, without fear of contradiction, that
they are the most polite and amiable, kind and courteous,
hospitable and charitable, happy and cheerful, contented
and frugal, tolerating and forbearing, extenuating and
forgiving people I have ever known, and the best and
most generous masters I ever had in my life. Yes!
"Russia, with all thy faults, I love thee still!"'

My informant I had known long, I can vouch for his
veracity, and I have not a doubt of the accuracy of his
narrative.

CHAPTER II.

THE URAL MOUNTAINS.

THE Ural mountains constitute an extensive range, stretching from the Gulf of Kara in the Arctic Ocean southward to about the paralell of 50°, throughout an, extent of 900 miles, with numerous lateral ridges, the aggregate of which is never under 30 miles in breadth, and in some parts reaches 120 miles.

The north division of the chain beyond the parallel 65_0 is covered with forests and morasses. The average elevation between the paralells 58° and 56° is only about 1350 feet, though the base on which the range rests has an average altitude of 900 feet above the level of the sea. The highest part of the range is to the north of this; but the highest summit is not more than 5000 feet.

The forests are a continuation of the forest zone extending through Norway, Sweden, Finland, and the Russian Governments of Olonetz, Archangel, Vologda, Viatka, Perm, and Ufa, and more immediately of that in the three latter Governments. Information in regard to the others has been embodied in volumes previously published,[*] while the forests in Ufa have been spoken of in the preceding part of this volume.

---

[*] *Forestry of Norway.*—In which are described in successive chapters the general features of the country. Details are given of the geographical distribution of forest trees followed by discussions of conditions by which this has been determined—heat, moisture, soil, and exposure. The effects of glacial action on the contour of the coun try are noticed, with accounts of existing glaciers and snow-fields. And information is supplied in regard to forest exploitation and the transport of timber, in regard to the export timber trade, to public instruction in sylviculture, and to forest administration, and to shipbuilding and shipping ; and,
Finland: Its Forests and Forest Management.
Forest Lands and Forestry of Northern Russia.

F

The Government of Viatka is conterminous with the Government of Vologda on the north, and is bounded by that of Perm on the east, which is also conterminous with the Government of Vologda. It has an area of nearly 54,000 square miles, of which many thousands are occupied by ramifications of the Ural mountains, and by marshes, and by immense forests. The soil is in general clayey, but there is a large tract of rich fertile mould on the banks of the Kama. The climate is cold, especially in the north; but the population, who are of the Finnish race, are diligent cultivators, and a considerable quantity of corn is exported. The export trade is not extensive, but amongst other articles of export are firewood, timber, tar, game, pottery, honey, and wax, and also copper and iron.

There are in the Government several navigable rivers; amongst others the Kama, the Viatka, the Tcheptza, and the Kilmes. Viatka, the capital of the Government, a town of 8000 inhabitants, is situated at the confluence of the Viatka river and the Klinoritza. Thence are sent to Archangel corn, flax, linseed oil, tallow, honey, and wax.

The Viatka, giving its name to the capital and to the Government, rises in the eastern part of the Government, and after a curved course of 500 miles, in which it passes Viatka, Orlov, Kotelnitch, Malinisch, and Mamadich, it flows into the Kama on its right bank, near to the last-mentioned town. Its principal affluents are the Kobra, the Letka, the Velekaia, and the Maloma, on its right bank; and the Tcheptza and Kilmes on the left.

I am informed that in the Governments of Perm and Viatka you find chiefly red pine, Dantzig and spruce fir, birch, larch, cedar, mountain ash, elder, aspen, lime, crab, and raspberry and black currant bushes, &c., all of them indigenous, and attaining to great magnitude, perfection, and beauty.

In the Government of Perm the area of Crown forests is

22,687,000 desiatins, of which 13,139,316 desiatins belong to the Crown, equivalent to 77·9 desiatins of the forests, or 45·1 desiatins per square verst of the land. The annual fellings in the Crown forests yield 6·7 cubic feet, and the revenue is 2·6 kopecs per desiatin.

This Government, bounded on the west by that of Viatka, and on the north by that of Vologda, is situated chiefly in European, but partly in Asiatic Russia. It has a reputed area of 128,978 square miles, and is intersected from north to south for above 450 miles by the great Ural chain of mountains, here from seven to seventy miles broad, and is in general a hilly country covered with vast impenetrable forests. The rivers on the west side of the Ural chain flow into the Kama, the tributary of the Volga, those on the east side of that chain fall for the most part into the Obi, which discharges itself into the Frozen Ocean. There are about 600 lakes scattered over the Government, most of them to the east of the Ural range.

The forests contain various animals, such as the sable and martin, which are hunted for their furs, and also bears and other beasts of prey. The south-eastern part of the Government is fertile and cultivated, producing rye, barley, oats, flax, and potatoes; but though the climate be warm in summer, cold winds from the mountains often blast the hopes of the husbandman, and the most of the country is much fitter for pasturage than tillage. The occupation of most of the inhabitants is pastoral, but about 100,000 are employed in connection with the mines, from which are obtained iron, copper, platinum, gold, silver, salt, marble, agates, and loadstone.

Perm, the capital of the Government, is situated at the confluence of the Jagashika with the Kama, which here flows with a swift current and a deep stream. It has a population of 10,000. The houses consist in general of wooden structures of a single storey, ranged round a quadrangular court, but there are several stone houses and public buildings.

The general control of the Ural mines is vested in a board located here.

In the Governments of Olonetz and Archangel the exploitation of forests has been largely determined by the demand for large timber for exportation to foreign lands, or to St. Petersburg. In the Government of Vologda and Viakta it has been largely determined by the demand for timber and firewood in the district, and in the interior of the country. In the Government of Perm it has been determined mainly by the demand for timber and for fuel in the mining operations, which have given its character to this region of the Ural.

It being the requirements of mining operations in the region which has given its character to the forest economy and exploitation of the forests existing there, we may glance at the history and development of these operations.

A writer on the Ural mountains in *Fullarton's Gazetteer* remarks in regard to the gold found in this region :—

'The continental tracts formerly so rich, as cited by Strabo, with the exception of the North Ural or country of the Arimaspès, whence the Scythian ores came, are no longer gold-bearing districts. The Scythian or Uralian tract had, in fact, remained unknown and unattended to from the classical age until this century, and so completely ignorant were the modern Russians of the existence of gold in the Ural mountains, or that they had in their hands the country which supplied so much gold to Greece and Rome, that excellent German miners had long worked the iron and copper mines of that chain before any gold veins were discovered. These also were worked as solid veins in the rock for some time before the accidental discovery of a small per centage of gold ore in the ancient alluvium or drift led to the superficial diggings, which produced at an infinitely less expense ten times the amount of produce of the mines in the solid rock near Ekaterineburg. All the energy displayed by the Russian miners having failed to augment the amount of Uralian gold, and as it has never much exceeded half-a-million sterling, the period is gradually arriving when the local depressions or basins of auriferous detritus of that region will be successively dug and washed out, and the Ural will then resemble many other countries in possessing actual mines of iron and copper, but merely a history of its gold. Russia, however, has also the golden key of all Eastern Siberia, in which various offsets of the Altai chain, chiefly those which, separating the rivers Lena, Jenisei, &c., stretch along the shores of the Baikal lake, have proved so very productive, that for some years they have afforded three millions sterling average, exclusive of the Ural. . . .

'In a paper read before the British Association, Sir R. Murchison points out the error into which some persons had fallen, that the Uralian mines were worked underground; the only small subterranean work is one near Ekaterineburg, which affords a very slight profit. All the other mines along the Ural chain, throughout 8° of lat. are simply diggings and washings which are made in the detritus or shingle accumulated on the slopes of the ridges and in the adjacent valleys, and, with one exception, are all upon the east side of the range. This phenomenon is a necessary result of the structure of the chain ; the older deposits through which the eruptive rocks have risen constituting chiefly the crest and east slopes of the chain, whilst the western slopes are occupied by deposits of younger or Permian age.'

In regard to the origin of these auriferous deposits the same writer states :—
' When the region of Permia was submerged beneath the sea, and the Permian deposits were in process of formation, the Ural mountains formed the rocky shore of a low continent, from which powerful streams poured into a western sea. That old continent contained iron and copper, but neither gold nor platinum; for traces of those

metals have never been found in the Permian *débris*. In
rocks still older—such as the carboniferous conglomerates
—there is no trace of gold; nor in rocks far younger, such
as certain tertiary grits. From these, and other reasons
equally strong, Sir Roderick Murchison concludes that the
Ural chain became auriferous during the most recent dis-
turbances by which it was affected, when its highest peaks
were thrown up, the present water-shed established, and
the greenstone, porphyries, syenitic granites, and other
comparatively recent igneous rocks, intruded through the
palæozoic rocks, along its eastern slopes ; in short, that gold
was one of the most recent mineral productions anterior to
the historic era, and coeval with mammoths and rhino-
ceroses. Their bones are seldom detected out of the line of
the gold-works ; and the Baskirs regard them with super-
stitious respect, saying to the Russian miners, " Take from
us our gold if you will ; but, for God's sake, leave us the
bones of our ancestors." Along with gigantic quadrupeds
are found the remains of the *Bos Urus*, now the only
survivor of this ancient *fauna*. A question of interest
arises from the total absence, on both flanks of the Ural,
of erratic blocks, and of any traces of those scratches,
groves, and polishings, which are considered, by the advocates of the glacial theory, to be proofs of the former
existence of glaciers. Its drift is all local and not transported ; and in the northern portion of the chain, between
60 and 65° of lat., no glaciers are found on peaks constantly covered with snow, and attaining an altitude
exceeding that of the highest mountains of the British
Isles. This absence of all the phenomena of glacial
action seems to exclude the possibility of the lower or flat
regions of Russia having been once invested in a cerement
of ice. The problem connected with the entombment of
mammalian remains in the gold alluvia, as well as in
alluvium generally, is difficult of solution, but by whatever
means the universal destruction of those great mammals,
during one particular period, may be attempted to be
explained, Sir Roderick answers, that it was owing,

in the district under consideration, including the low regions extending from each flank of the Ural, to an elevation whereby a change to a colder climate was effected. To the general view of Baron Humboldt, that the richest gold deposits are those which are derived from ridges having a meridian direction, M. Erman is opposed; but Sir Roderick is of opinion that it is a fact that the greatest quantity of gold ore has been obtained from chains having a nearer relation to north and south than to equatorial or east and west directions, due perhaps to the general form of the chief masses of land, and the prevailing strike of the palæozoic rocks. . . .

'Comparing California with the Ural, Sir Roderick shows that there is a very great coincidence of mineralogical structure, and that with these *constants* the same results obtain; the chief distinction consisting in the apparently larger proportion of gold in the detritus of the newly-discovered deposits in California than in those of the Ural. More recently, Sir Roderick and other geologists have observed a striking resemblance between the geology of the Ural chain and that of the Blue mountain ranges in Australia, which run, in a general line, not far from the meridian, through 30 degrees of latitude in Tasmania and New Holland, and New Guinea, having their highest points at an altitude of from 5000 to 6000 feet above the sea ; with an axis of chloritic and talcose schist, and quartzites, with occasional limestones of Silurian age, in which occur metallic ores and gold in veins of quartz. Moreover, granitic rocks of a comparatively younger age break through them. As on the flanks of the Ural, the carboniferous formation reposes, so in Australia occurs the very same order of deposits. Sir Roderick, therefore, anticipated the extraordinary discovery of gold in the Australian continent, thinking it most highly probable that, besides the lead and copper which exist in the Blue mountain ranges, auriferous sands would be found in the rivers flowing from them. In respect of other phenomena, the dividing ranges of New Holland are similar to the Ural,

with the exception that the slope in this hemisphere is to
the west and the escapement edges of the deposits to the
east. So far as has been yet ascertained, the drift of the
Ural mountains seems to have its parallel in that of
Australia, which is all local, and much of it fluviatile,
deposited at the ancient mouths of the present rivers when
the country was at a lower level. The phenomena pointed
out by Captain Sturt render it far from improbable that
the interior depressed area of Australia is of similar
character to the great Aralo-Caspian country. From these
and other facts communicated to the Geological Society,
Sir Roderick predicted the probable mineral wealth of
Australia, and in a letter addressed to Sir C. Lemon, and
published in the *Philisophical Magazine*, was the first to
advise that a person well acquainted with the washing of
mineral sands should be sent out to Australia, speculating
on the probability of auriferous alluvia being abundant in
that region.

'In the paper read before the British Association
already referred to, Sir Roderick adverts to the distinctions
between such surface mining operations as those of Siberia,
California, and the Brazils, and those works in which,
besides the ores of silver, copper, &c., gold had also been
extracted from the veins in the solid or parent rock, as in
Mexico. Sir Roderick also traces the history of gold and
its development as known to the ancients and our ancestors of the middle ages; and shows that in all regions
where rocks similar to those he had described occurred,
there gold had been found in more or less quantities; and
that just in proportion to the time that a country has been
civilised has the extraction and produce of the precious
metal diminished ; so that in many tracts where it formerly
prevailed to some extent, it has been either worked out
or the mines have been almost forgotten.'

'Considering the short space of time which has elapsed
since the conquest of Siberia,' writes Sir Roderick
Murchison, 'and up to how recent a time these mountain

tracts remained in a state of impenetrable forest inhabited by idolatrous Voguls and Ostiaks upon the north, and Mohammedan Baskirs on the south, we ought rather to feel astonishment at the rate with which the region has been cleared and civilised through the introduction of European manners and mining industry. When Peter the Great, with a keen perception of the surest methods of advancing his empire, selected the first Demidoff to explore the iron ores of these mountains, he laid the foundation of the great native mineral wealth which now so conspicuously distinguishes Russia from all the surrounding nations. The earliest mining establishments or *zavods* planted by that great sovereign are still the centres of activity, and have served as models after which numerous other works have been formed, both by the Government and private speculators. In the days of Pallas, geology was so little understood (a few gold mines only being known, and a great portion of the country unreclaimed), that the descriptions of the great naturalist are chiefly to be viewed as vivid portraits of living nature; as such, indeed, his observations have well stood the test of time, and small gleanings only have remained for those who followed him. Since that time, the Russian miners, learning their first lesson from foreigners, have become a well-informed class, independent of extraneous aid, and their directors (officers of the imperial school of mines) have described the lithological and mineral characters of the country, around their respective posts, with great fidelity.'

'The axis, or central portion of the chain, consists to a great extent of talcose schists, or chlorite and quarzite, ancient sedimentary strata, for the most part in a highly metamorphic condition, in consequence of numerous syenitic and trap rocks, but on account of the presence of certain organic remains, traceable at intervals in limestones to the silurian series. Along the eastern flank, the most accessible by reason of the mining establishments, the strata are also greatly altered by the prevalence of igneous rocks; it was only along the western flank that Sir

Roderick and his companions were enabled to establish a
clear succession of carboniferous, devonian, and silurian
deposits. True granite is of very rare occurrence along
the axis of the chain, and has at a comparatively recent
period burst through the eastern dislocations. The
periods of dislocation, the change of relative level of land
and water, and of the protusion of igneous rocks, appear
to have been phenomena repeated at different geological
epochs. From the occurrence of cupriferous minerals
diffused throughout the Permian strata, Sir Roderick
infers that anterior to the deposition of those beds,
metallic veins must have existed in the Ural mountains;
and from the abundance of the remains of terrestrial
plants in the same deposits, that the chain must have been
raised to a certain extent above the level of the then existing
ocean. Subsequent periods of disruption are proved by
the lines of disturbance in the Permian series on the
immediate flank of the Ural range, and connected
with dislocations which have affected them. The patches
of Jurassic rocks at the north and south extremities of
the range, are considered to have been subsequently
desiccated, and the absence of strata of that age throughout the great mass of the chain, or for 12° of latitude, to
prove that it was constantly above the level of the sea
during the Jurassic epoch. Between that period and the
accumulation of the gold alluvia, there are no signs of
any great changes in the physical structure of the Ural
range, and the only deposits assignable to that interval
are certain trachytic grits and beds of lignite, which, it is
conceived, may have been formed in lakes. On the west
side of the chain the order of the metalliferous rocks is
best developed; but it is on the east igneous slopes that
the miner is best repaid by ores. Sir Roderick concludes
that " the widely-spread cupriferous deposits of Permia,
which occupy all the low country to the west of these
mountains, have been derived from pre-existing eastern
lands, upon which the plants and vegetables enclosed in
the Permian conglomerates must have grown. Judging

from its composition—it is entirely made up of fragments of ancient Uralian rocks—the great Permian deposit must have been accumulated, not only after the completion of the silurian, devonian, and carboniferous systems, but after their consolidation, and either after or during their mineralisation with copper ores. This is a clear and undeniable conclusion, at which the field-geologist who has examined this region arrives ; for, in whatever parallel of latitude he may trace this ancient detritus, he invariably finds it to be more coarse and metalliferous as it approaches the mountains from which its materials have been derived, whilst in receding from them, such mineral matter (always in the form of deposit, and never in the condition of veins) as regularly dies away and is lost in marine marls, sand, and limestone. But if the Ural mountains were, as we contend they must have been, the source whence all these cupriferous sediments, as well as detritus and fossil vegetables, were supplied, very different indeed must have been their former outline from that which now prevails ; for on the western slope of the axis down which the waters now flow into Permia, there are no great vein-stores and original sources from which such *débris* could have been derived. All the spots where the largest veins, masses, and original centres of copper ore occur, whether at Bogoslofsk, Nijny Taglisk, Gumeshefsk, and Polofsk, south of Miask, or other and intermediate places, are on *the eastern side of the chief ridge.* Supposing that these mines were in the process of forming, or having been formed, were undergoing destruction, during an era in which the land had assumed its present outline, almost every cupriferous particle and drop of water impregnated with or transporting such mineral matter must have descended into the adjacent low country of Siberia. By no natural agency could any considerable quantity of such coarse materials be now carried to the low countries on the west, between which and all the great copper sources which are known lies the ridge of the Ural range. Now, as all the cupriferous detritus has been carried to the western flank of the mountains, and not a particle of it into the low country of Siberia, it follows that by far the greatest variation in physical outline which the region has undergone— one by which a lofty wall was thrown up between Permia and the orginal copper-sites of the Ural range—took place at a period posterior to the formation of the Permian deposits." '

CHAPTER III.

METALLURGY.

'ABOUT 180 years ago,' writes Barry in 1870, 'there lived two blacksmiths at Tula, who had heard of the immense quantities of iron that lay, scarcely covered by the soil, throughout the Empire ; of the abundant forests, that seemed to offer an inexhaustible supply of fuel ; and of the advantages offered by the Government to any who would take in hand the development of those stores of wealth,

'The names of the two blacksmiths, Demidoff and Botachoff, are now household words through the length and breadth of the Empire. Both were men of great genius, and extraordinary energy ; when one looks at the work they did, and considers the difficulties they had to contend with, we do not know whether most to admire the magnitude and boldness of their conceptions, or the patient energy and perseverance of their conduct. They both prospered nearly alike.

'Demidoff, branching out from his first works, which he established at Neviansk, in the mouth of the Ural, had soon availed himself of every spot where water could be collected, and he founded an ironworks there.

'No authentic record, I believe, exists of the precise number of foundries which he built ; but Botachoff, who, it is known, followed closely in his wake, left behind him twenty-five large works, extending over something like a million and a half acres, and employing a population of upwards of fifty thousand souls.

'After the death of Demidoff and Botachoff their pro- perties were cut up and divided, constantly increased by their successors, and again partitioned in another genera-

tiou; and so the iron industry has spread from these two
fountain heads to its present great proportions. Copper
mining was not undertaken in the country until a later
date. The now famous mine of Nijni Tagil, the first of
any importance of any that was opened, was not worked
on till 1814. It was on the site of one of Demidoff's
original works, and is owned by the descendants ef Demidoff's family to this day. It was soon discovered that all
the country on the Asiatic side of the Ural mountains,
from a point a long way to the north of Tagil to another
close upon Orenburg in the south, abounded with copper
ore. A number of mines were quickly opened on this
line of country, and many copper works erected.

'The immediate descendants of the two great blacksmiths, of Demidoff and of Botachoff, found themselves
enormously wealthy beyond all necessity of enterprise or
exertion. They acquired great influence in the Empire,
were raised to the nobility, and appointed to high offices
of State by the Imperial Government. Their attention
was thus withdrawn from the sources of their greatness,
and the management of their mines, left to the hands of
subordinates, deteriorated. As time rolled on, other
people began to open copper mines and iron foundries in
competition with theirs; prices and profits were reduced,
but the two families, accustomed to greatness, neither
applied themselves to maintain the efficiency of their
mines, nor to reduce their personal expenditure, which
exceeded the income they derived from them. They soon
began to borrow large sums on the mortgage of their
properties, chiefly to the Government, but in part to anybody who would make them a loan, and thus many of
their works came into the hands of the Government.

'The families of the Demidoffs and Botachoffs, in their
system of borrowing at all hands, were soon embarrassed
to meet the payments of interest as they fell due; and
the Government readily took advantage of their default,
by taking the estates and works of the insolvent families
into its own management; nominally still for the benefit

of the proprietors, but in the first place for the satisfaction of the claims of the Government, under the control of a Committee of Tutelage, or so called " Tutor;" and the issue has been that many of them have become Government works.'

Of these works I may state, as is stated by Barry, that they are, or were, of a character peculiar to the country, and such as are not to be met with elsewhere.
' Many of the establishments extend their operations over a space containing from three-quarters of a million to a million and a-half English acres ; and 'erect their works here and there where a favourable site exists, thus forming little principalities containing numerous villages, which are entirely supported by the labour of the mines ; and in the olden times the " Barrin " lived in almost princely style—in a palace surrounded by highly ornamental gardens and extensive parks, laid out with the most excellent taste.   In his gardens were hot-houses, vineries, and orange-houses, erected at great expense.   Frequently he had a private theatre of his own, a band of music in constant attendance ; and I know of at least one of the ironmasters of the last generation, who supported a company of actors and actresses, collected from among his own mujiks, whom he sent to St. Petersburg and Moscow to be educated expressly for his own stage.   Such a man, in the days of serfdom, had all the state and authority of a monarch, enjoying unlimited and irresponsible power among his servile dependents.   Of course, the condition of these last was regulated by the character or caprice of the master : some were cruel ; but, on the other hand, some governed their people with a kindness and discretion wonderful to think of in men brought up as they had been.'

Connected with this development of metallurgical and manufacturing operations by Demidoff and Botachoff, occurred the development of mining operations in the Urals.

With a view to introducing and establishing in Russia
the arts and manufactories of western and central Europe,
mines in this region and elsewhere were wrought, and manufactories of various kinds were established and carried on,
at Government expense, first, by Peter the Great, and subsequently by some of his successors on the throne. Accurate
accounts of the expenditure and of the proceeds of these
were kept. These often, I may say almost always, showed
that there was less profit than loss resulting from them.
But notwithstanding this they were maintained in full
operation as being likely to prove remunerative by developing the resources of the Empire, and the energies of the
population even while continued at a loss.

Some of them are still carried on at a great loss; but
the policy adopted and followed now appears to be to
abandon them in favour of manufactories carried on by
private enterprise, with or without aid in the provision
of capital by the Government, at such rate of interest as
may be agreed upon.

A friend and correspondent who resided in this district
for many years, and was well acquainted with the various
industries and works carried on on the Ural, wrote to
me :—

'As I have heard from men born in the locality, and
from officials connected with these zavods, of their first
formation and establishment, I may briefly refer to this.
There is a splendid monument erected at Nijni Tagil to
the memory of the first Ural Demidoff, who was a black-
smith, and sent up there by Peter the Great to teach how
to make iron. And, like his great master, he has created
for himself an imperishable name. It needs " no sculptor's
art or studied urn " to perpetuate Demidoff's fame on the
Ural.

'He commenced his first operations at Neviansk. It is
the most quaint, grotesque, and interesting place on the
Ural, and has quite an antiquated look, pretty nearly as
he left it. I have been there, and seen them still making

iron which you can twist about like lead without breaking
it; and they are still making horse-shoes, nails, spades, trays,
and boxes, said to be the best in Russia, if not in the world.
If fibre and ductility are to be the test, this iron will bear
comparison with any Swedish or Low Moor iron you can
produce.   I have seen their iron twisted and tied into all
kinds of beautiful knots like twine, and this of all sizes, up
to three quarters of an inch diameter.   And I have seen
their sheet-iron as thin as paper, as smooth and as bright
as a mirror, and weighing only a quarter of a pound to the
square foot.   All the old zavods which were built by him,
both those built for Government and those built for private
owners, are still acknowledged by all competent authorities
to have been laid out with great practical skill and judgment, generally at the confluence of two or more streams
which drain all the water from the surrounding hills for
water supply and water power.   He picked out the nar-
rowest, and otherwise most eligible spot, between two banks,
and there he made his dams, stretching right across the
river, and these of various heights according to the natural
formation of the vale, some of them having a fall of thirty
feet.   Then he erected the works below the dams, naming
them after the river near which they stood.   These water
dams are now large and beautiful lakes, some of them
thirty versts long and ten wide, four times the area of
Loch Lomond.

  ' Had those vast forests, those extensive lakes, those
inexhaustible mines and mountains of ore, some of them
containing 80 per cent. of pure iron, been in the hands of
our countrymen, they would have been worth more than
the mines of Peru, California, and Australia, all put
together ; and the proprietors would not have been, as
they are now, in the slough of despond.

  ' Some of these estates are as large as Yorkshire ; the
Government of Perm is as large as England, the whole
Ural region is larger than all the British isles put
together.

  ' It is very interesting to watch them let off these lakes

G

in the spring; and start off their caravans for the Nijni fair. Allow me to describe it as well as I can.

'They build on the banks of the water-course, below the works, large rude flat-bottomed barges. These are lowered into the narrow stream in winter, and laden with iron. Now when all is ready in spring, and the lakes are full, or filling, by the rapidly thawing snow, there is a grand and usual ceremony—prayers, incense, blessing with holy water, and all the rest of it.

'Vodky and pies for the lower orders, champagne and zakaska for the upper ten, as all the work people and employés, the owners, and many of their lady and gentlemen friends assemble, some from long distances, to see the sport and lend *eclat* to the occasion. At a signal from some principal, the floodgates are lifted, when out bounds the surging foaming billows; and when the stream is sufficiently swollen, the first barge is let go amidst a deafening shout for a few minutes; then all is hushed, and immediately all heads are bobbing up and down, and there is seen such a commotion, as hundreds of arms are waving about like windmill vanes, while all are crossing themselves during their short and silent prayers. Let us hope they will bring the God-speed they invoke—Why not? —the guiding and steering of those barges through all the rapids, sharp bends, and sudden turns of the chasovai, hundreds of them one after another,—twenty or thirty from a zavod, till they fall into Kama and are comparatively safe.

'I thought of the tide which, embraced at the flood, bears down to fortune ; and those huge unweildy boats must catch the right moment, float down with the ebbing stream, or, be left high and dry on the banks till next season : a very expensive and inconvenient thing when it happens.

'I have often admired this simple, primitive, and effective way of conveying their merchandise from these remote districts, for it only costs 16 kopecs a pood from the Ural to the great Nijni fair, though they have to

tug up the Volga from the mouth of the Kama, a little
below Kazan. Railways cannot compete with them. 1500
versts for 15 kopecs the pood !
'I am sorry I don't know exactly the total amount of
metal sent annually from the Ural ; but I have been told
that the firms of Steinbak, Demidoff, Stroganoff, Druz-
hinine, Gubine, and others, deliver in Nijni from 300,000
to 500,000 poods each ; but I believe if those mines were in
the hands of English puddlers they would turn out as
many tons as the Russians now do poods.'

At Nijni Tagilsk, or lower Tagilsk, near to the fort,
on the eastern slope of the Urals, are famous mines and
works belonging to Demidoff. They were visited by Dr
Lansdell, who tells :—
'There had been a fire in the town on the night preceding our arrival; and in seven hours seventy-eight
houses had been burnt. Pieces of smoking wood were
still flying about. The common people attributed the fire
to incendiaries, such as escaped prisoners, who hoped to
profit by the turmoil, and find an occasion for plunder ;
but more thoughtful people traced it to accidental causes.
Demidoff's workmen had been called out at night to assist
as firemen, and were in consequence resting. We could
not, therefore, see everything in motion, but enough was
visible to make it clear that they were carrying on
enormous metallurgical operations. One of the remarkable things to be noticed was a surface mine of magnetic
iron ore, blasted and dug out in terraces, carted down by
horses and taken to the furnace, where the ore proves so
rich that it yields 68 per cent. of iron. We also descended
a copper mine, the mineral from which yields 5 per cent.
of metal. We were dressed for the occasion in top-boots,
leather hats, and appropriate blouses and trousers, each
carrying a lamp, and thus by ladders we descended one
shaft of 600 feet and came up another, the water meanwhile
trickling upon us freely. At the bottom of the mine they
were erecting an English machine for pumping 80 cubic

feet of water.per minute to the surface. In the engine-
room two men at a time spend eight hours daily, for which
they each receive in money about fifteen pence. We prom-
ised ourselves, as a great feature in the descent of the
copper-mine, the seeing of malachite in its natural state ;
and we were not disappointed. The captain took us
through long galleries of timber beams, and then to the
spots where the miners had been working. Here, by the
light of our lamps, the pieces of green mineral could be
clearly seen, and we had the pleasure of digging them out
with a pick, and bringing them away as specimens. The
price of malachite at the mine is six shillings a Russian
pound, if in moderate-sized pieces ; twenty shillings when
the lumps are large, but only two shillings if they are
small.

  ' Besides these copper and magnetic iron mines, they
have others of maganese iron ore, which contains 64 per
cent. of binoxide of maganese, the peroxide being sold at
the rate of about eighteen shillings per hundredweight.
Specimens of these, and other minerals of great interest to
the geologist, are exhibited in a museum not far from the
works.

  ' Among the remarkable things to be seen at these
hives of industry were—a machine for drawing water by a
cord from a copper-mine two miles off, a steam-hammer of
seven tons weight, an iron furnace of 10,000 cubic feet
dimensions, said to be the largest high furnace for *wood*
in the world, and a machine for splitting their fuel wood,
of which they burn annually 100,000 *sajens*—that is to
say, a 325 feet cube, or, roughly speaking, a pile of logs
twice as big as St. Paul's Cathedral.*

  ' They make steel for Sheffield, and can do castings up
to more than 30 tons in weight. Their iron is excelled in
quality, I believe, only by that of Dannemora. They have
eleven *zavods*, or " works," of which eight are connected

---

* What extent of land must be cleared to furnish such an quantity of fuel I know not,
but the railways of Central Russia are said to consume yearly the timber off 90,000 acres
of forest—an area, that is, about the size of Rutlandshire.

with iron. But perhaps a better idea can be formed of
their vastness by the mention of the number of persons
employed, which amounts to 30,000. I heard also 40,000,
and both numbers were from heads of departments; but
probably the latter estimate includes carters, labourers,
and perhaps even women. The Demidoffs pay annually,
by way of rates and taxes—to the Commune, £5000; the
Church, £1,500; schools, £2,500; poor and aged, £3000;
together with other sums, amounting in all to about
£20,000 a year. Wages, as compared with those in
England, appeared low. Common workmen receive from
7½d to 1s a day, puddlers 3s, and those in the welding furnace 4s, whilst good rollers receive from 3s 6d to 6s. It
should be observed, however, that they all have houses, rent
free, with the piece of land they formerly occupied as serfs.

'Before the emancipation, the riches of the Demidoffs
were counted in the phrase then usual in Russia as
amounting to 56,000 souls.* A small church, built on
the crest of a hill, was pointed out as having been built
by the serfs in memory of their freedom; and I was glad
to hear from the director, Mr Wohlstadt (by whom we
were courteously entertained), that since the emancipation
the men work better and better, knowing, I presume,
when serfs, that idleness would be repaid with something
not much worse than a beating; whereas now they know
they may be discharged.

'We slept at the club; and in the morning, before
leaving, visited the Demidoff hospital, upon which, and
upon institutions of a similar kind, the proprietors spend
nearly £4000 a year. The dimensions of the rooms were
such as to allow three cubic *sajens*, or 1,200 cubic feet, of
air for each of the patients, of whom there were 120 at the
time of our visit. Many fractured and amputated limbs
were seen dressed with gypsum, alcohol, and camphor;
but the most extraordinary thing was a machine in the
director's private room, in which he placed frozen human

* That is men, or at least *males*; for male children are called " souls," but female
children never,

brains, and for scientific purposes cut them in very thin
slices to photograph. The photographs are to be purchased in Paris.'

According to a report by Professor N. A. Jossa, Professor
of Metallurgy in the School of Mines in St. Petersburg,
the total products in 1880 were as follows:—

	Poods.*	Lbs.
Gold, -	2641	29
Platinum, ...	179	36
Silver, ...	616	28
Lead, ...	69,947	
Copper, ...	195,578	
Zinc, ...	237	800
Wrought Iron, . . .	17,940	531
Cast Iron, ...	3208	536
Steel, ...	18,761	298
Graphite none ; there are mountains of it on the Ural.		
Coal, anthracite and charcoal used,	200,942	523
Nefta (Naphtha), . . .	21,947	995
Crome Ore, - . . .	503	503
Marganitz (Manganese), . .	614	549
Sulphur, ...	5	500
Distilled Salt, . . .	47,571	916
Glubed Salt, - . . .	66	650

Number of people employed in the miners' gold
washings, blast and puddling furnaces, rolling mills,
tilting hammers, &c., 283,414. Total power employed,
steam and water H.P. (Horsepower ?), 76,090.

In a lecture by Professor Jossa on the manufacture of
pig-iron, delivered before the Royal Society of Engineers,
there is supplied information in regard to the use of charcoal
employed.   From a *résumé* of this lecture by Mr C. Kirk-
shof, C.E., published in the Journal of the United States
Association of Charcoal Ironworkers, it appears that in this
lecture Professor Jossa enters into an elabarate account of
the ore deposits of the country, and the character of the
ores, which embrace almost every variety known to iron-
masters ; but all that it is necessary to state is that the
supply is ample for present needs, and is sure to remain
so, even if taxed by a much larger industry. 'As a general

---

* The pood is equal to 40 lbs, Russia ; 36 lbs, avoirdupois.

thing, the fuel used is charcoal Some works employ wood and charcoal, and in the south-western portion of the country iron is smelted with mineral fuel. Generally the ores are prepared by roasting and breaking, and only in rare instances, as at Kiselovo, are they washed. Roasting is usually done in heaps in the vicinity of the mines. Kilns are rarely used. The fuel is almost exclusively wood, the quantity being, for instance, 35 cubic feet per 2·5 metric tons, at Gora Blagodat, in roasting in heaps; and 35 cubic feet per 3·145 metric tons in Raschett kilns, at Visokaja-Gora. Only at some of the works, where the roasting kilns are near the furnaces, as at Malceff and Stroganoff, waste gas is used. Latterly, vertical kilns, built after a Styrian (Austrian) model, have been put up at Katakov, for furnace gas; and at several Government furnaces for smelting brown hematites, an apparatus, designed by Moskvin, has been constructed. It consists of a series of cast-iron segments placed above the tunnel-head, from which the ore, roasted by the flame issuing from the furnace, is dropped into it at a red heat, by loosening the keys which hold the segments together. The ore is generally broken by hand, but at some works the cheaper method of using a Blake crusher has been adopted.

'The pine or birch wood generally available is converted into charcoal in vertical meilers, as in the north of Russia, and in Poland; sometimes, as in the Moskow district, horizontal meilers are employed. Two kinds of kilns, the Mosolovski, having a capacity of 850 to 5,500 cubic feet, and the Schwarz kiln, ranging from 4,250 to 10,000 cubic feet, are used—the former chiefly in the north-east, and the latter in Finland and Olonec. The circumstance that the supplies of charcoal are rarely stored under cover is a great disadvantage. The measure for charcoal is the basket, holding from 49 to 152 cubic feet, the standard being 71* cubic feet in north-eastern Russia and Finland. In Central Russia, the unit is the " Tschetwert" of 7† cubic feet, and

---

* Equal to about 45 bushels of 2,748 cubic inches.
† Equal to 4 4-10 bushels.

in Poland a basket of 46 cubic feet.* Wood is charged in
some places in Central Russia and Finland, in a dried or
charred state, the pieces being split and cut to 13-inch
lengths.

'The furnaces are, as a rule, old, with massive masonry
of brick or stone, the shaft and boshes being circular, while
the hearth is rectangular. The lower part of the lining is
usually built of stone, which material is often used also for
boshes and shaft. Brick is not common. They generally
have an open top, the gases either being allowed to escape
from the tunnel head or being taken off by a flue. The
front, too, is open in most cases, only a few furnaces in
Central Russia, in the Ural mountains, and in Poland,
having a closed front. The number of tuyeres is two or
three, and sometimes only one; their diameter, however,
is large. The blast is, in most instances, cold, and the
pressure low. The height and diameter of the furnaces
vary. In Finland and Olonec they are only from 29·5 to
34 feet high; in the Ural mountains the height is generally 49 feet and upwards, while the average in Central
Russia is 39 feet. Modern furnaces have from 3 to 12
tuyeres, the masonry of the hearth is water-jacketed, and
their section is either round or ellipitical, according to the
Raschett model, and the shafts are built free. Hearth and
shaft are made of brick, but often, as at the Peskov works,
the Scotch system has been adopted, while in other cases
the furnaces, like the Nijni Tagilsk No. 3, and the
Nijni Saldinsk, the Büttgenbach system has been
chosen. Modern furnaces all have hot blast stoves heated
by gas, the furnace top being closed by the Langen, Parry,
or Fröhlich charging apparatus. In many cases the waste
gases are also used for making steam, as at Kuschava
Tagilsk, and occasionally also for roasting ore. The construction of the hot blast stoves varies. In the Ural
mountains the Wasseralfingen pipes are put up above
the level of the tunnel head, in Central Russia the Calder
stove yields blast heated to 150 degrees C. (302° F.), whilst

---

* Equal to 29 bushels.

modern Westphalian and Swedish stoves, as built at Tagilsk, the Katov stove with suspended pipes, and the Whitwell or Cowper stoves yield much higher temperatures. As a rule the older blowing engines are vertical, and have one cylinder, while those more recently put up have two. Oscillating engines are rarely built; one at Nijni Tagilsk is of this type. The pressure is low, being between 2·95 and 3·94 inches. Only a few modern blowing engines like that at Nijni Saldinsk furnish blast at a pressure of 4·91 to 6·88 inches.* They are, as a rule, driven by water power, and steam-engines have been erected only at some furnaces to act as a reserve in case of scarcity of water.

'The furnaces are so built that ore and fuel are brought to the top by means of a bridge; but in plants recently put up, as in Southern Russia, and at Nijni Saldinsk, power or pneumatic hoists are used. Generally ore and fuel is charged by hand, and only occasionally by barrows. The charge is so chosen as to produce a slag approaching a bisilicate. In the Ural mountains grey or mottled pig, of exceptional purity, and suitable for the manufacture of steel, is obtained from pure magnetites, while foundry pig is made with the aid of fluxes. At Jurjazan, spiegeleisen, holding from 10 to 12 per cent. of maganese, is produced from brown ores from Visokaja Gora, mixed with maganese ores. Ferromaganese is only made at Tagilsk. In the north of Russia, as at Kamensk-Kasla, excellent foundry pig is made from pure brown iron ores, and at Peskov a similar grade is produced from specular ores. In Central Russia, Olonec, and Poland, castings are made direct from the furnace. In Finland, at Abo, and Njuland, an excellent grade of refinery pig is produced from iron glance brought by sea from Sweden, while the works of Central Russia yield only metal containing phosphorus.

'The following table gives the dimensions, number of tuyeres, temperature, and pressure of blast, charges smelted, iron produced, fuel consumed, and quality of iron:—

---

* An inch of mercury equals about one half-pound pressure.

DIMENSIONS AND WORKING RESULTS OF RUSSIAN BLAST FURNACES.

Name of Furnace.	Height—feet.	Dimensions of bosh—feet.	Dimensions of Top—feet.	Dimensions of Hearth—feet.	Capacity of Furnace—cubic feet.	Number of Tuyeres.	Diameter of Tuyeres—inches.	Pressure of Blast—inches.	Temperature of Blast—Degrees Fahr.	Average production per 24 hrs—met. tns.
Furnaces Smelting Magnetites.										
1. Nijni Tagilsk, No. 3 a,	53	18.75×10	18×9	3.25	8,052	12	0.75 to 1.97	1.50 to 5.43	Cold	26.0
" " b,						12	0.75 to 1.97	1.50 to 5.43	140 to 572	28.4
" " c,						12	1.97	3.04 to 4.40	392	20.7
2. Kuschwinsk No. 3,	49	14	7	3	3,425	4	2.9 to 3.5	1.5 to 2.5	Cold	11.0
3. Sucha-Gora (1875-1876),	57	14	14	3.5	7,525	4	2.0 to 2.4	2.0	266	10.6
Furnaces Smelting Brown Iron Ores and Magnetites.										
4. New Schajlansk,	41	13.5	7	2.3	3,077	2	2.7 to 3.1	3.1	572	16.5
5. Vochnje-Isjetsk,	35	10.75	7.6	2.3	1,765	1	3.3	1.7 to 2.2	Cold	12.6
6. Kyuovsk (1876-1877),	46	12.25	8.7	2.3	2,895	3	—	2.5 to 2.7	158 to 212	9.0
Furnaces Smelting Red and Brown Iron Ores.										
7. Archjangjel-Paschiisk,	49.5	14.25	7	2.5	3,708	4	2.7	0.7 to 0.9	Cold	10
Furnaces Smelting Brown Iron Ores.										
8. Kaslinsk (1877),	36.25	11	6.5	2.3	1,600	3	3.5	8.0 to 2.0	Cold	18.0
9. Jurjazan (1878),	50	12.25	7	3.5	3,143	3	2.0 to 7.9	8.0	572	19.1
10. Satkinsk (1875-1887),	42	16.3×9.7	14×7.25	2.1	3,814	8	1.5	3.0 to 3.7	Cold	19.5
11. Kysjelovsk No. 2, (1876-1877),	46.3	11.7	7	2.3	2,790	5	0.7 to 1.5	3.5 to 3.9	Cold	9.0
12. Taschinsk (1877),	37.25	12.25	7.6	2.3	2,295	2	2.7 to 2.9	3.9 to 4.9	482	15.5
13. Ljudinov No. 1, (1876-1877),	38	10.75	7	3.1	2,048	2	1.7 to 3.5	2.0	176 to 212	6.8
Furnaces Smelting Specular and Brown Iron Ores.										
14. Kuvinsk (Natalia Furnace),	40.5	10.9	7	2.7	2,613	3	2.6	1.7 to 2.0	Cold	9.5
15. Peskov, a,	39.0	12	7	2.3	2,401	2	2.7	1.0 to 3.9	Cold	
" b,	39.0	12	7	2.3	2,401	2	2.5	1.0 to 2.9	Cold	
16. Wiksunsk,	35	11.7	3.25	3.0	1,978	2	2.0 to 2.2	1.5	698	8.1
Furnaces Smelting Bog Iron Ores.										
17. Walasminsk (1878),	32.25	9	6.5	2	1,271	2	2.0	1.0 to 2.0	Cold	4.9
18. Mohko (1877),	40.6	9.7	6.75	2.5	2,578	2	3.0	2.0	357	8.5

RUSSIAN BLAST FURNACES—CONTINUED.

Name of Furnace.	Max. production per 24 hrs.—metric tons	100 parts pig if on yield per cent.	100 parts pig if charge yield per cent.	Ore—metric tons	Flux—metric tons	Charge—metric tons	Charco'l metric tons	Wood—cubic ft.	Pine.	Fir.	Birch.	Mixed.	Cub. capacity ℔ ton produced per 24 hours.	Grade of Pig.
Furnaces Smelting Magnetites.														
1. Nijni Tagilsk, No. 3 a,	48 2	65 0	65 0	1 54	0 34	1 54	1 05			7 7			307	Grey
" " b,		65 c	60 1	1 54	0 15	1 68	0 93				10 1		248	"
" " c,		66 0	60 1	1 50	0 06	1 65	1 22					8 6	385	"
2. Kuschwinsk No. 3,	15 1	57 0	55 9	1 75	0 12	1 81	1 31		6 9	5 4			308	Bessemer
3. Sucha-Gora (1875-1876),		40 8	38 9	2 45		2 57	1 59						706	Bessemer
Furnaces Smelting Brown Iron Ores and Magnetites.														
4. New Schajtansk,	15 5	51 6	45 7	1 94	0 27	2 23	1 12			4 4	4 4		183	Gr'y & mot
5. Vochnje-Isjetsk,		54 0	49 5	1 85	0 16	2 01	1 23		5 6	7 9	7 5		137	"
6. Kynovsk (1876-1877),		49 9	45 4	2 00	0 90	2 20	1 69						314	"
Furnaces Smelting Red and Brown Iron Ores.														
7. Arehjangjel-Pachiisk,	14 8	45 0	39 0	2 22	0 34	2 58	1 83	6 46	5 6	3 1			364	Mill pig
Furnaces Smelting Brown Iron Ores.														
8. Kaslinsk (1877),	22 1	51 6	47 9	1 93	0 16	2 09	1 34				6 2	13 7	85	Mill pig
9. Jurjazan (1878),		60 0	56 7	1 65	0 06	1 71	0 76					8 5	39	Grey
10. Satkinsk (1875-1877),	13 1	50 0	45 4	1 99	0 22	2 21	1 05				7 1	6 9	201	Foundry
11. Kysjelovsk No. 2, (1876-1877),	19 6	51 6	44 6	1 94	0 30	2 24	1 89						307	Mill
12. Taschinsk (1877),	8 8	43 9	40 7	2 28	0 18	2 46	1 60						123	Mottled
13. Ljiudinov No. 1 (1876-1877),		50 0	41 7	2 20	0 40	2 49	0 90						307	Foundry
Furnaces Smelting Specular and Brown Iron Ores.														
14. Kuvinsk (Natalia Furnace),	9 9	44 72	40 5	2 23	0 22	2 45	1 61		4 3		1 1		272	Mill
15. Kcakov, a,	9 9								5 4				—	Mill
" b,	7 4								4 7				—	Foundry
16. Wiksunsk,	11 5								2 5			5 8	208	Grey
Furnaces Smelting Bog Iron Ores.														
17. Walsaminsk (1879),		30 5	27 9	3 28	0 35	3 63	1 37						258	Foundry
18. Mohko, (1877),	9 8	34 6	30 8	2 89	0 35	3 24	0 96	41	4 1			2 5	261	Foundry

' If the work of the three furnaces smelting magnetites is examined, it will be noticed that Nijni Tagilsk, No. 3, has the best, and Sucha-Gora the worst record, as the latter requires 706 feet of cubical capacity per ton of iron, compared to 248 to 385 for the former. This is apparently due to the fact that the ore is richer, which contributes also to a diminished consumption of fuel. Some furnaces, as those of Ljudinov and Möhko, are run with wood and charcoal. It is interesting to compare the results of some Russian furnaces, as to cost of production and consumption of fuel, with furnaces elsewhere in Europe. The nearest approach to the Russian conditions are found at the Längs works, Sweden, where magnetites holding from 51 to 52 per cent. of iron are smelted with pine charcoal. The furnace in question is 49.25 feet high, has a 7.5 foot bosh, and has a cubical capacity of 3,110 feet. The blast is carried up to 410, and to 482 degrees F., and blowing with 2.36-inch pressure, turns out 1.6 tons of iron per day. It carries, for 71 cubic feet of charcoal, 0.671 tons of burden, the consumption of fuel being 75 parts, by weight, of the 100 parts of iron made. The cubical capacity of furnace per ton of iron per day is 1,921 cubic feet. The Nijni Tagilsk furnace, though larger than the Längs furnace, and working ores holding 60 per cent. of iron, takes 93 parts of coarcoal per 100 of iron, and 2,479 cubic feet of capacity per ton of iron per day of 24 hours.

' In a similar way, the furnaces smelting the good and rich brown hematites of the southern Ural district may be compared with those of Styria and Carinthia, which work the roasted specular ores of the Alpine ore deposits. The furnaces of the Austrian Alps are remarkable, as compared with those of Russia, for smaller dimensions, and for comparatively higher production, at a lower consumption of fuel. They are generally from 33 to 47 feet high, and have a capacity of 1,400 to 1,750 cubic feet. The Vordernberg furnaces requires 64 to 78 cubic feet of capacity per ton of production, using 237 to 247 cubic feet of charcoal per ton of iron, or 80 parts, by weight, per 100 parts of iron. Aside from other circumstances, this may be due to the fact that the bosbes are steep, the hearths more capacious, the tops smaller, and the fronts are closed. It should be remembered, too, that the Austrian furnaces smelt well roasted ores with good dry charcoal and hot blast.

' Besides improving the lines of their furnaces and using hotter blast, the iron-masters of Russia are urged by Prof. Jossa to reform their methods of manufacturing charcoal. At present, the usual yield with the different methods is as follows : With the Ural meiler, 50 to 64 per cent. for fir, and 40 to 52 for green wood (i. e., oak, birch, &c.) ; in the Suksunk meilers, 58 to 76 per cent. for fir, and 51 to 60 per cent. for green wood ; in Tyrolese meilers, 60 to 72 per cent. ; and in kilns, 60 to 72 per cent.* Even though the yield is greater in kilns, their use is not advocated, because of higher first cost and more expensive maintenance, as compared with meilers, and because as high a yield can be reached with the latter. In order to obtain the best results in meilers, the use of wood felled at the wrong time must be abandoned, and the unskilled labour must be replaced by efficient men. In order to accomplish that end it would be well to found charcoal workmen's schools, as the Swedish Konteret has done. By using other fuel for mills and forges, and placing them in a position to obtain coal or peat, the charcoal supply for the furnaces might be increased. Peat, too, might be used as a blast furnace fuel, as is done at Vordernburg, Austria, where two parts of

---

* These percentages evidently refer to the volume of charcoal obtained from a given volume of wood. Reducing them to the number of bushels of 2,748 cubic inches, obtained from a cord of 128 cubic feet, and making no allowance for intersticial space, we obtain the following results :—
The Ural meiler yields 40 to 51 bushels per cord of fir, and 32 to 44 bushels per cord of green wood. The Suksunk meiler produces 49 to 65 bushels per cord of fir, and 41 to 48 bushels per cord of green wood. The Tyrolese meiler and the kilns give 48 to 61 bushels per cord.
From these results we should presume that the calculation was made on the actual volume of wood, intersticial space being deducted. Assuming the space between sticks at 40 per cent. of the volume of a wood pile, the Ural meilers yield 19 to 30 bushels, the Suksunk meilers 25 to 39 bushels, and the Tyrolese meilers and kilns 29 to 37 bushels per cord.

compressed peat and one part, by weight, of charcoal is
charged, 2.8 parts of peat being considered equivalent to
one part of charcoal.

'Prof. Jossa also gives some details of the manufacture
of ferromanganese at one of the Nijni Tagilsk charcoal
furnaces. The ores used at the Nijni Tagilsk furnace
have the following composition :—

LEBJAZEJ MANGANESE ORE.

Mn_3O_4,	...	...	...	...	... 64.5
Fe_3O_4,	...	...	...	...	... 20.2
SiO_2, ...	...	...	...	..	... 10.2

VISOKAJA-GORA MAGNETITE.

Fe^3O_4,	...	...	...	...	... 90.0
Mn_3O_4,	...	...	...	...	... 0.6
SiO_2,	...	...	...	...	... 5.0
Al_2O_3,	...	...	...	...	... 3.0
CaO CO_2,	...	...	...	...	.. 0.9
P, ...	..	...	...	...	... 0.02

'The charge consists of 40 parts of well-roasted iron ore,
90 parts of manganese ore, 5 parts of calcined lime, and
some cinder from previous smelting. For every 126 pounds
of charge, 6.3 cubic feet of charcoal are used, and with
blast heated to 250° to 300° C., and 5.2 inches pressure,
60 charges are put through in 24 hours, the production
being from 1 to 1.5 tons of metal, having a percentage of
manganese ranging from 40 to 50 per cent. When the
furnace is working well, the cinder is yellowish-green and
fluid. As soon as the hearth is much worn out, the charge
is changed, and a pig rich in silicon is aimed at. On a
charge of 126 pounds of charcoal, the burden is 110 pounds
of magnetite and 17.6 pounds of quartz sand, the pig made
running from 3.7 to 9.5 per cent. of silicon. Recently,
silicon ferromanganese has been made, containing 40 to
45 per cent. of manganese, 3 to 7 per cent of silicon, 6 to
8 per cent. of carbon, and 40 to 45 per cent. of iron. First
iron rich in silicon is aimed at, and as soon as the furnace
is in good working order the burden on 126 pounds of

charcoal is 13.2 pounds of silicon pig, 90.4 pounds of manganese ore, 4.4 pounds of lime, 8.4 pounds of cinder, and up to 19.8 pounds of quartz sand. In 24 hours, 40 charges pass through the furnace, yielding 1.1 to 1.2 tons of metal. The cinder has the following composition :—

				I.	II.
SiO_2,	...	...	...	... 40.75	38.85
Al_2O_3,	...	...	...	... 13.44	12.13
MnO	...	...	...	... 31.06	33.40
FeO,	...	...	...	... 1.21	1.22
CaO,	...	...	...	... 11.43	11.99
MgO,	...	...	...	... 1.56	1.86'

There are three terms in frequent use in connection with manufacturing industries in Russia—fabrique, usine, and zavod. Zavod appears to be the designation given to large establishments for the founding and casting of metals, and the manufacture of large machinery. Fabrique is applied to what in English might be designated a manufactory, being applicable to manufactories of cloth, chemical preparations, candlemaking, coachbuilding, and other variations of carpentry and smith work. Usine seems to be applied to smelting works in connection with mines.'

CHAPTER IV.

FORESTS.

In a preceding chapter mention has been made of the extent and character of the forests of the Urals, and of the form of exploitation carried out in these being determined largely by the demand for timber and firewood required by the mining and metallurgical works of the district.

Many of these manufactories, while in the hands of the Government, were subsidised by grants of lands, of serfs, and of forests or of forest rights. The administration of all such forests is kept apart from the administration of the Crown forests by the Minister of Imperial Domains ; and it, together with the administration of the forests in Poland, is placed under the supervision of the Minister of Finance.

By an English engineer, who had been employed in connection with ironworks in the interior, to whom I applied for explicit information, I was informed that if in any Government it was desired to erect works for the smelting or manufacture of iron the proposal was submitted to the Governor of the province, who, after an official inspection and report, granted permission for the erection of the works, and for the felling of trees to be used as fuel in accordance with prescribed conditions, including provision for Government inspection, and provision for replenishing the forest, the felling of which was limited to something like a twenty-fifth part annually. He could not say whether the proportion related to the area, or to the cubic contents of the forest, but considered it more likely to be the former.

The wood is required in smelting, and melting, and casting and manufacturing much of the metallic produce of the mines, and as fuel for the production of steam as a motive power in the works and in the transport of products.

In the various works which were established the most was made, or I should rather say an endeavour was made to make the most, of what motive power could be obtained from running water; but it was found impossible even thus to meet all the requirements of the case. Steam had to be employed, and besides the consumption of wood to produce this motive power, which could only be thus applied at the expense of fuel, fuel was required to produce heat, both for smelting ore and for working metal.

When making enquiry in Russia some years ago in regard to the effects upon the forests of this phase of forest economy, and the working of the system, my attention was directed by an English engineer, who was one of my correspondents, to the following statement on the subject which had appeared shortly before in *The Journal of Science, Metals, and Manufactures* :—

' Animated by the desire of developing every possible resource of the Empire which he saw might achieve such enormous power and dimensions, Peter the Great, in the year 1700, commissioned two men—Botachoff and Demidoff—to inspect and report upon the facilities which were offered in the country for the establishment of centres for the manufacture of iron.

' These men went their ways, and filled with the spirit of their master, devoted their faculties to the task, with results that, considering the disadvantages under which they laboured, were really marvellous. Perhaps the grandest monument of the energy and genius of these two men are to be found in the gigantic dams which they constructed to keep the water up. To this day these constructions strike the beholder with admiration and amazement at the indomitableness and perseverance which they displayed. These may fairly be considered the most wonderful dams that were ever built.

H

'Demidoff, availing himself of water-power wherever it was procurable, soon very considerably extended his operations, and before long, finding the Ural too circumscribed for his energy, and having exhausted all the productive places thereabouts, he carried the works far into Siberia, ceasing only at a point some two thousand versts distant from Neviansk, where he first commenced his work.

'While Demidoff was thus closely employed in the north, Botachoff was not less assiduous in prosecuting his labours in the centre and south of Russia; in fact, he had one advantage which his fellow-workman, Demidoff, did not possess—viz., that of procuring labour with greater ease and cheapness. On the other hand, however, he had to contend with an evil to which the latter was a stranger, that is to say, the levying of black mail upon him and his works by the robber chiefs of the Mouron woods, in proximity to which he had commenced his operations. Nevertheless, he covered every available spot with ironworks, and it is said that the iron that he floated down the Oka, at Nijni-Novgorod, was often exchanged for its equivalent weight in copper money. In this last respect, that of disposing of his manufactures, Botachoff possessed an advantage denied to Demidoff, as the latter was only able to convey his iron down the Kama and Volga once a year, while the former continued his trafficking all the year round. To the works established by Botachoff Russia was first indebted for the manufacture of sheet iron, which is at the present day, as it always has been, quite the specialty of her productions.

'At the establishment of this industry, in certain districts in Russia a peculiar tenure of the works and lands, known as "possession right," was introduced; and as it is somewhat unique in character, and has not been without its effects on the development of the works, it may be well briefly to describe it here. It is only right, however, to state at the same time that the Government never fully realised the hurtful and obstructive nature of the principle;

but we believe that a plan will shortly be put into action by which the properties shall become freehold, and thus the development of the industry will not be fettered, as we shall see immediately that it has previously been, by the "possession right."

'Under this tenure an exclusive right was granted to cut down wood within certain prescribed limits, and for this privilege a tax on all the iron made was imposed. The purpose of this tax, and the supervision of the works which arose out of it, were no doubt needful, and were not without their recommendation, for, as will be readily understood, some regulations were necessary to prevent the complete denudation of the land of the forests which covered it, and the Government inspection was intended to accomplish this. But such legislation naturally restricted all mining and smelting operations, for no new furnaces and no extension of the works could be introduced without obtaining permission from Government. There were several arbitrary regulations with reference to a variety of petty details, such as the procuring of the wood necessary for fuel, &c., and which, in removing from the proprietors the sense of ownership, and in taxing their productions, naturally disinclined them for extended operations, and thus kept the industry within confined limits, and in a languid condition.'

Several of the arrangements referred to will subsequently come under consideration. Meanwhile, the depressed condition of the mining industry here spoken of may demand attention, in connection with other evils which have tended to produce the state of things in this respect which is spoken of.

CHAPTER V.

DEPRESSED CONDITION OF MINING, SMELTING, AND MANUFACTURING ESTABLISHMENTS.

FOR some three thousand years it has been a proverb—
'It is naught, it is naught, saith the buyer; but when he
is gone his way he boasteth.' Constant complaints are
heard that the smelting and manufacturing works in the
Ural district have become unremunerative.

On this point one of my correspondents, on whose statements I rely with implicit confidence, wrote to me :—

'After having travelled over a good part of the Ural,
and been at nearly all the principal iron and copper mines
and works, including those belonging to Steinbok, Demidoff, Stroganoff, Sukazanct, Belizovskoi, Druzheinine,
Gubina, and many others, besides the Government
works at Nijni Isetsky, Miask, Zolotaust, Kushvinsky,
Kuyash, Satkinsky, Berozoffsky, and others, I found all in
one and the same tale ; nearly all of them are unremunerative, and, with few exceptions, all of them in debt and
irredeemably mortgaged to the Government, and the Imperial mines and zavods nearly all stopped or closing. You
can buy any of them for an old song—by paying for 32
years 6 per cent. on the original outlay of capital, then the
property becomes yours out and out for ever, and the only
drawback, the only hindrance, is no fuel—the one great
desideratum is want of timber ; no more forests to cut
down, except at very great distances from the works.

'I have heard a great deal about the virgin forests in
Russia, but though I have been in many Governments,
chiefly in the forest zone, and from zavod to zavod on
the Ural, both on the Asiatic and on the European side of
the mountains, yet I never saw them or ever had the

chance to pass through them. They say, "Oh ! they are farther back." Aye, there's the rub. It is because they are so far back that they are not come-at-able. It is just because all the available woods are cut down except those that are still young and not worth the felling within reasonably accessible distances from the works and centres of life and business. And it is this rapid, reckless diminution of their forests, and the increasing scarcity of charcoal fuel that now brings up the prime cost of their iron to almost a prohibitory figure in so far as competition with the foreign market in Nijni-Novgorod fair is concerned. A few years back, when iron was up at such exorbitant fancy prices, they did make money, in some cases cent. per cent.; but when it is at its normal value they cannot sell their iron or copper at the fair at anything like a remunerative price, and yet the sheet-iron from some of the principal works is said to be the best in the world, for one main reason, because it is made entirely by charcoal from beginning to end, and it is this that gives it such a rare softness and such a fine polish as it possesses. When they begin to make puddled iron from their anthracite coal they will have no chance at all unless they entirely prohibit the importation of iron, for which prohibition many of them have been crying for a long time. But surely that is not to be thought of; and even if it were granted nine-tenths of the owners of these mines have no funds wherewith to effect the requisite reconstruction of the furnaces: they are all so deeply involved, I may say inextricably involved, with the Government, by loans which they have obtained. Shall I describe how they manage this business ?

'The beginning of their working year is immediately after the great Nijni fair, held in the end of August. Then all their labouring hands are ready to re-commence work, having returned to the zavods from their month of hay harvesting on their own account. At each zavod there is then made out an estimate of the quantity of iron and copper to be made in the course of the ensuing year; of how much charcoal they will require; how many square decatins of timber they intend to cut down on the estate for fuel, according to a given plan and specification—but the quantity hewn, and the locality operated upon, is thereafter fixed, just as it happens afterwards to suit their convenience.

' The Imperial Bank in Ekaterineburg makes to them an advance of working capital upon the basis of that project, in order that the zavods may be kept going to find bread and employment for all people living and depending entirely on these mining operations in the district.

' There is a mining engineer in the Government service appointed to look after the Imperial interests, to receive and store the iron as it is made, to see that the Government money is rightly disbursed, and to see to the whole business being properly conducted, well managed, and honestly worked out. The whole scheme seems feasible enough if fairly carried on, and one would think the Imperial Bank ought to receive the 6 per cent. per annum required for the cash so liberally confided to the owner until the amount is reimbursed by the sale of the iron at the next annual fair. But there is invariably a deficit, there being always large items of extraordinary and unaccountable expenses, so that instead of the finances of the zavod improving, a debt goes on accumulating year by year, until it happens, in accordance with the proverb, " The last straw breaks the camel's back." The Government will advance no more money, so all comes to a dead lock, and this, perhaps, not for the first time. And what is the cause of this deplorable state of things? How have these debts been made, and why do they increase like a snowball with every turn, even under official control and duly authorised supervision? The answer is ready—the reason of all this is very obvious! The one great parasite eating into the vitals of any and every Russian undertaking is speculation. Then to change the figure—the most powerful brake which operates here to prevent the success and development of every enterprise, trade, or business, is constant petty theiving—men purloining little by little at every chance, abstracting and defrauding in every possible way. And this is a delinquency common to all concerned, from the highest to the lowest, with all of them, always in proportion to the opportunities they have and the position they occupy. It is a saying, "There is honour among theives," and this may account for the phenomenon that Russian officials are very clannish in their way. They all stick to one another like glue; they stand by, screen and help one another in every muddle and scrape. No doubt the law of self-preservation is the motive power, so that among them all transactions are made to look square and presentable by cooked books and garbled accounts, apparently technically right, though morally wrong.

'Allow me to illustrate this. I have known several estate stewards—"unjust stewards," invested with full power of attorney—having only 600 roubles a year salary, who, it has been said, have made their fortunes of one, two, and three hundred thousand roubles in a few years; and I have heard of officials set to watch over them receiving from these very men—mis-managing directors—5000 and 6000 roubles a year as "palm oil," as it is called, to induce them to sit quietly at home, to sign all papers they are required to sign, to hold their tongues, and to ask no questions. Of course, you cannot prove that it is so, as these nefarious practices are done in such a secret, hole-and-corner sort of way, that there is no external evidence left liable to exposure; but the "Jeremy Diddler" thimble-rigging is patent to all: as these very *blind* watchmen spend on their splendid establishments, and in high living, gambling, &c., more thousands annually than they get hundreds in the shape of Government pay. And if you say anything about it to anyone, or even to the parties most intimately concerned, it is only met with a grin and a shrug, and "Stcho daelat!" (What is to be done!) They tell you that they are not the only ones, nor are they altogether in fault. They palliate their misconduct by

urging that they have to maintain the rank, position, and
appearance of a gentleman on the income of an artisan.
But, like the man that pled as an excuse for adulterating
his goods, that "he must live," to whom the complainant
replied, "I don't see any necessity for that in the least,"
so is it with them.

'Allow me to relate an anecdote bearing on this sweeping assertion of mine, and I believe it to be strictly true,
as I had it as a fact from an English engineer formerly
employed at these very works, in regard to which I have
to supply you with details. Suffice it here to say : Here,
on the Ural, is a very large estate, upwards of 400 square
versts, said to be very rich, almost inexhaustibly so, in
water, timber, iron, copper, gold, nickel, plumbago, and
goodness knows what besides, having twenty different
zavods on the estates. These works and mines are called
"zavods," not towns or villages, but some of them
contain 35,000 inhabitants.

'The proprietor of these estates died a few years ago,
and left them in a very prosperous condition, without a
kopec of debt, and under administration till his two sons
should come of age; but he unfortunately, too confidingly,
made his wife chief executrix, and his steward joint executor.
Well, this beautiful young widow, a Moscow merchant's
daughter, very shortly thereafter married a fine, handsome
man, a General, and, as is often the case, a poor, beggarly
spendthrift, a gambler, a libertine, and a bankrupt. They
spent for a time a gay life, chiefly in London and
Paris, and their plenipotentiary on the Ural had got to
supply them with 250,000 roubles a year. No matter how
he does it, or what he does, or where the money comes
from, so long as there is a constant and regular remittance
they ask no questions, and never look at, much less look
into, the reports and accounts that are sent. They estimated these at what they were worth. They had a pretty
strong and settled idea that the one in full possession was
very comfortably feathering his own nest all the while and
all the same, without ever saying "By your leave."

'Now, while this is going on, as this managing steward has a full power of attorney, and has by hook or by crook to meet the constant harrying cry of "Give! Give!" and perhaps to stave off the evil day, and to escape temporary detection, as everything is going the wrong way, he pledges and mortgages till at last the old cow is dry, and will yield no more, having been drained to the tune of 4,000,000 roubles.

'Well, when this rich stream at length ceases to flow, he is at last compelled to make a clean breast of it, and let them know that it is of no use attempting to pump any more water out of a dry well. This soon brings the gay couple home again, leaving many tradesmen's bills unsettled abroad. Of course the stewardship alone is to blame; and the steward has to bear all the approbium of mismanagement, rascality, and all the rest of it. But it turned out in this case that the man in charge was not altogether and alone in fault; and he left their service, not only a poor man, but like the one in "Timon of Athens," he had ruined himself by his endeavours to stave off the impending blow from the heads of his late beloved master's sons.

'As the next steward did not succeed in finding the needful any better than did the last, nor even so well, this soon brought the General, the husband of the proprietrix, upon the spot, with plenary powers from his wife, and having also got himself appointed administrator by the Court for the protection of the widow and orphans. How he protected the widow and orphans you shall hear. There was no more iron to pawn, no more money to be borrowed, no more estates to mortgage, as these had been sequestrated by the Government long before; but, in the language of the old play, this virtuous step-father says, "Money I want, and money I'll have. If you don't give me money, I'll sweep you all into the grave." I will give you a saying I have often heard ironically among the Russians, but there was a grim reality in this case—" Seal unbroken, lock secure, store-house empty, everything in the best condition. Glory be to God!" This exactly describes the state of things on this occasion, for when the time had come for the iron to be sent off to the Nijni fair, many magazines which should have been full of pledged iron, supposed to be safely reposing under lock and seal, were found to be empty. There was a hue and cry you[may be sure; but the horse was flown, though the stable door had not been unlocked; and to whom could they bring home the guilt? Nobody had either done it or seen it done. Oh, no! All concerned protested their innocence, though it was quite palpable that the rascals had broken open the stores, removed the iron into other magazines, and repledged to the bank their own iron.

'Of course all the officials and leading men of the place were implicated; and as the authorities must make some show and fuss, and give some one in charge, the Prekazchik was made the scapegoat and held responsible; though there is no doubt he had been acting under orders and promises of protection, and that all parties concerned had connived at the action if they had not criminally participated in it, or in sharing the proceeds of it. It is a saying, "You must set a thief to catch a thief." That may be so. But you can't get a thief to set about catching himself; so to this day there has been no clue to the perpetrators of this barefaced robbery.

'Let us pursue this story a little further, and then we shall see what sort of honour there is among thieves on the Ural.

'When there was a criminal investigation appointed, this said Prekazchik took the alarm and thought he would make his treasure sure by confiding his mysterious accumulations (said to be upwards of 100,000 roubles, though he never had more than 60 roubles per month of salary) to an old friend and accomplice, a very wealthy and respectable merchant, a dealer in iron, but it must be mentioned he sold a very great deal more iron than he was known to buy. After the steward had done this he again took the alarm, thinking this professed friend to whom he had entrusted his ill-gotten gains might prove a rotten stick, so he thought his money would be safer in the hands of an Englishman, a merchant residing in his own zavod, and to him he gave a written order to receive back from his doubtful friend 30,000 roubles as a first instalment. But the old fox was not to be caught napping; and when that order or letter was presented this honourable thief friend exclaimed, " What does the man mean? Is he gone mad! If he do not retract his words, and that in writing, I'll prosecute him for libel; and I'll call upon him to show how he comes to be possessed of so much money. I never had a rouble of his! What has he to show that I ever had?" He (the Prekazchik) saw that he had jumped out of the frying-pan into the fire; and as he had no legal evidence which he could or durst produce, he had to submit and collapse, while his former friend spread out further his branches like a green bay tree. And notwithstanding that it is a generally understood thing how this man has acquired his great wealth, yet every one bows and wishes Ivan Trefeemovitch good morrow with all apparent deference. So much for the commercial morality of the Ural, and the brigand-like honour among Siberians.

'I have referred to this disreputable affair in perhaps, for you, too lengthened detail; but I have done so to show you the undercurrent influence which is always at work. The motive power that pervades and moves all classes is self-interest—self first and self last—no matter how secured, and often by subterfuges that will not bear the light of day. And then they bear themselves with a boldness and effrontery which is inexplicable. They make a joke and a laugh of it. They treat it altogether so; and they have a string of characteristic proverbs which govern them in their sharp practices such as the following: " Simplicity is worse than duplicity;" " A fool will lose his own money as well as yours; but the cunning fellow that has brains enough to make money for himself has sense enough to make, at the same time, some for his employer; but it unfortunately happens that his own profits are always in his thoughts firstly, while the interests of his employer are secondly and occasionally;" "The silver key is the only picklock that will open every door in Russia,"—yes, but it sometimes requires a very large one of gold; "The creaking of a wheel may be stopped by well greasing;" "You can't handle gold dust without some of it sticking to your fingers;" "If you can't cheat you can't sell, at least you had better not;" "It is not the wrong you do that condemns you, but the exposure;" "See that you never have any other witness but yourself." These are not a tithe of what I have heard among them, merchants and chinovnicks alike, but they are enough to show how their barometer stands in matters of honesty.

'I have already made a passing reference to the timber business, and as wood is to the Ural what coal is to England, let us get back to the forests for a little.

'I was most intimately acquainted with the chief forester at these works, and as they are of the largest and the most important in the Ural mountains they may stand for a mirror for all the rest; and the reflection wont be a very distorted one in any case.

'He was a German, and I believe a conscientious, industrious man, more especially considering that he was a Russian German, and had been educated and brought up in the country.

'He laboured to bring the smelting operations of these furnaces into a system, and the felling of timber for charcoal into something like a proportional ratio to the growth of new wood.

'He lived in these wilds for weeks and months together, and it is no joke to do so amongst bears and wolves, mosquitoes, hornets, and all the rest of them. Let any one try it and he will find a sore trial put upon his coolness, courage, temper, and patience.

'He was the first to cut through these woodlands proper

roads which divided and portioned them out in lots and squares for each zavod. By his calculation they would be 60 years in clearing off all the timber on the estate; and by that time he reckoned that the young forests would be sufficiently grown to allow and pay for felling again, supposing the zavods not to exceed the manufacture of their usual quantity of iron (350,000 poods a year), including all kinds of sheet plate, flat, square, round, &c.

'This superintendent of woods and forests put up signboards and finger posts on the roads to each lot and square, allowing each zavod to cut down only according to number, rule, and plan. It was a great improvement upon the old happy-go-lucky style of working; and if they and all the other zavods had always worked on that principle there would have been fuel amply sufficient for all time to come.'

I may interrupt the statement of my friend to state that such was probably the best arrangement which could have been made at the time and in the circumstances. It was in accordance with the celebrated French Forest Ordinance of 1669—the system of exploitation known in France as *La Methode à Tire et Aire*. But this, unhappily, has its defects as well as its advantages. These will in due time appear. Suffice it here to remark, that by the time referred to in the statements supplied to me the forests in the immediate vicinity of many, if not of all the zavods, had been entirely consumed.

My correspondent goes on to say:—

'When the mountain would not come to Mahomet, Mahomet could go to the mountain. But these forests and zavods will be a long time before they approximately approach each other again, so we conclude that all profitable smelting operation is now out of the question, and that they are getting to the fag end of their manufacture of charcoal iron. Such difficulties are they labouring under that a blunt Lancashire friend of mine compared it to ploughing with dogs.

'Had Englishmen had possession of those splendid

minos and estates thoy would long ago have put down
tramways intersecting all parts, by which would have been
brought up the ore and the fuel, especially from the
remote parts, at a much less cost. But it is too late now
for the owners to do so, as few of them have got the
spare cash necessary for even such a small improvement
as this; and the patience and help of Government has
been all used up a long time since. And no wonder,
when the debt amounts to 8,000,000 roubles, as in this
one case it does. English capitalists would have bought
up these very works a long time back if it had not been
for the crippling, paralysing effect of authorised regulations. The red tape is drawn too tight to admit of any
legitimate expansion, and a Briton must have elbow room.'

The foregoing is a saddening picture of mining operations in the Ural range. I have no reason to suppose it
is exaggerated in any of its points. I accept it as credible
and correct. It is in accordance with much which I have
heard in regard to such matters. The salient points of
importance to students of forest scenes are these:—There
has been a reckless consumption of forests in supplying
fuel for smelting ore. The ore is not exhausted, but the
fuel which was of easy access has been consumed. The
operations carried on have not proved continuously profitable to the proprietors; but this is attributable largely, if
not mainly, to their living beyond their income and to
others fattening on the products of the works. Could forests
be restored the work might be prosecuted with vigour and
possibly with profit. If not, if this is to be done other
fuel must be found.

My informant goes on to say:—
'The only zavods said to be in a healthy condition are
those of Verkny Isetsky, Bueluembaeff, and Kishteem,
belonging to Steinbok, Stroganoff, and Drazheinine. When
I was at Nijni Tagilsk, Demidoff's works, twelve years ago,
even firewood and charcoal were then scarce and dear.

They are expecting the new "mining railway" to bring up coal from Perm. But it remains to be seen whether it will benefit any but the works of Demidoff and Stroganoff, through which it runs, as it will never do to convey coal over those mountainous bad roads by carts and horses such as they have, 25 poods being a load.

'That was not the railway which the merchants and inhabitants of the Ural and Siberia wanted. They want to join the two great arteries of European and Asiatic Russia, the Kama and the Tobol, expecting that this will expand the Siberian trade. But even that will never pay at present, as there are only some 300,000 passengers passing over the Ural mountains in the year, and about 8,000,000 poods of merchandise.'

The failure of mining operations here to prove permanently remunerative is largely attributable to the failure of the supply of wood required in smelting, in melting, and heating the metal, and in the production of motive power in the absence of such power attained from the fall of water.

In regard to the motive power which is thus produced my correspondent writes :—

'Now you must know when I was in that remote district any new enterprise—the erection of any new mill, manufactory, or establishment of any kind requiring steam power was strictly prohibited by an old law, they say solely to prevent the exhaustion of the Government forests.

'Private landowners are also interdicted by authority from felling and selling timber of their estates. It can only be consumed in their own zavods for building, heating, and smelting purposes. The people belonging to and living on the works have their own woods told off for their separate use by right, and under the care and management, of the Commune.

'As a proof of this, there was a large stearine and soap manufactory erected near Ekaterineburg, at the cost of I

am afraid to say how many million roubles—I think it
was eight. It was brought to a standstill not many years
ago, and all sold off for not more than a tenth of what it
cost, and all because—no fuel, and none to be got for love
or money by them; bribery could not even help them
here.

'There is in Russia red tapeism enough in any conscience!
But how does it work? I was called to examine a boiler
at a certain manufactory in Ekaterineburg, and there I
saw lying a little turf and a great deal of firewood. I
inquired, "What is turf doing here; you are not burning
turf?" "Actually, no; ostensibly, yes. And that turf lies
there as a proof, when needed, to satisfy official inquiry.
But the paper roubles necessary to bandage the eyes and
stop the mouths of dangerous creatures costs us 4000
roubles a year to make them willingly insensible to the
fact that we are feeding our boiler with one vegetable
product instead of another." "Then why not get turf-
making machinery out from England and always burn
turf?" "Because we could not and cannot get the permission. They (that is the authorities) would say, if we
open a door for turf timber will escape through in unknown quantities." It was not doing so then! It is
because everything must be in black and white that those
that are well posted up can succeed so cleverly in making
black look white, It is a saying, "That what can't speak
can't lie." But in the interior, far from the executive,
dumb-lying is most general, systematic, and convenient.
The Russians have a maxim, "If you live in a wood you
must be content to dwell with wolves." Now the owner
of this establishment thought he would end this unpleasant state of things, as he was always in hot water, and
as he never knew or could rely upon the future, or secure
himself against a more extensive application of the screw,
till all should be torn away and his work shut up.

'He went to St. Petersburg; spent a great deal of time
and money endeavouring to obtain from headquarters a
concession or the permission to buy and use timber,

legally paying all dues, &c. But all that he could do was
—he secured for all parties in that neighbouroood the
privilege to consume 300 cubic fathom of wood a year;
and that only as an auxilliary to those works already
established possessing water power. But on no account
must any new works requiring steam power be erected.
And this concession he only received through the kind
intercession of the Empress. He was what we may call
church warden of her private chapel.

' Allow me a passing reference to this man not intimately
bearing on this subject matter. I think I could write a
book about him, and I think you will acknowledge by-and-
by he was worth a better tribute than I can pay him.
What I am about to relate I had from his own lips.
His grandfather was originally a serf in Rostoff. He
bought his own freedom, he then made himself a merchant, and left his family 9,000,000 roubles. That's
something for a mujik to do, no matter how he has done
it! I have his venerable daguerrotype taken when he was
90 years of age. He (the grandson) told me that their
house at one time employed 50,000 hands all round; that
they had passed through their books 135,000,000 I think it
was ; that they used to sell 450,000 poods of tallow a year —
I am afraid to say how many million sheep they knocked
on the head annually; that they had given away 350,000
roubles for the building of churches, schools, and charitable
institutions; that they had lost 850,000 roubles on bad
debts, and yet they never brought a case into court; that
they had been robbed incalculably by stewards, agents, and
employés, and never had prosecuted one. When they had
several millions in the bank his nephew had gambled it all
away. And at last his gay wife deserted him in his adver-
sity; and yet he forgave her and pensioned her off. With
tears streaming down his cheeks he said to me in my own
house, " If I am a Christian I must imitate my Divine
Lord and Master, who expiring on the Cross exclaimed,
Father forgive them, they know not what they do." Let
his God and our God judge that man what sort of a

I

Christian he was, not we! And now for the conclusion of the life of this truly good man.

'In 1872, as I was returning home I met him in the Post Hotel at Perm, when he said to me, "The saddest calamity of all has happened to me now. I am going to bury my dear and only brother, and we have yet to quarrel. Yes; for 50 years it has always been Yes, Yes, with us; and now I have received a telegram that he is dying."

'But it was otherwise determined. The reported death of his brother had so preyed upon his mind that he only arrived in Rostoff to die. He was taken and the other left — left to struggle on — left to carry his brother's remains to the family burying-place, while that brother winged his flight to the better land, where there are no unfaithful partners, and where no thieves break through and steal.'

Everything comprised in this little sketch is in keeping with much which I have heard in regard to Russian merchants—Russian roguery—Russian piety—and in regard to the wealth and extensive manufacturing and commercial operations of many who, belonging to the communal class of the population of the villages, have given themselves to mercantile pursuits. Without trenching on stores of anecdotes which from time to time I have heard forty or forty-five years ago, but in regard to which I am unable now to state who was my informant, or to vouch for my recollecting the precise terms in which they were told, I shall have occasion to bring forward many like narratives to these in making use in this chapter, or in some subsequent chapter, of material which my friend and correspondent has placed at my service.

In circumstances such as have been detailed, wrong-doing in any way and every way abounding, the alleged depression of many smelting and manufacturing establishments in the district need not excite great surprise, and even when it was attributable directly to the failure of an abundant supply of fuel from the forests; this it may be possible to trace to like abuses.

CHAPTER VI.

FOREST EXPLOITATION.

FROM different allusions which have been made in preceding statements to the exploitation of the forests, the produce of which is so necessary to the smelting of ores and the manipulation of metals, it may be gathered that this exploitation is conducted not by what is known in France as *Jardinage*, as in Northern Russia, details of which have been given in *Introduction to the Study of Modern Forest Economy*, pp. 137-138, in the *French Forest Ordinance of 1669, with Historical Sketch of Previous Treatment of Forests in France,** pp. 35-39, and in *Forest Lands and Forestry of Northern Russia*, pp. 89-100; nor by what is known in France as *Furetage*, as in some extensive forests in the Government of Ufa, details of which have been given in a preceding chapter of this volume [ante pp. 31-40], and in *Introduction to the Study of Modern Forest Economy;* but by what is known in France as *La Methode à Tire et Aire*, details of which are given in the afore-cited *Introduction to the Study of Modern Forest Economy*, pp. 138-153, and the *French Forest Ordinance of 1669*, pp. 40-44. I employ the French terminology because, as I have intimated above [ante p. 38], I do not happen to know any English terms applicable to the operations referred to of which I could make use while desirous of distinguishing things which differ.

---

* *French Forest Ordinance of 1669, with Historical Sketch of Previous Treatment of Forests in France.*—The early history of forests in France is given, with details of devastations of these going on in the first half of the seventeenth century ; with a translation of the Ordinance of 1669, which is the basis of modern forest economy ; and notices of forest exploitation in *Jardinage*, in *La Methode à Tire et Aire*, and in *La Methode des Compartiments.*

In the exploitation of a forest according to *La Methode à Tire et Aire,* when it was practised in France and in Germany previous to the introduction of forest exploitation, in accordance with the advanced forest science of the day, beside which it has become antiquated, the number of years which the trees would require to grow to reach the age at which they should be felled, whether coppice wood or timber were desired, was divided into some one or other of the factors of this number; and the forest was divided into a corresponding number of portions, one of which was felled in the course of one of the lesser periods, in the expectation that each in turn would be again covered with trees of the desired age by the time the cycle of fellings was completed.

The initiation of this method of exploitation did not originate in France or in Germany in the promulgation of what is known as the famous Ordinance of 1669. This Ordinance assumes it as being already known and practised. But to this Ordinance we are indebted for its introduction into many lands.

In the *Introduction to the Study of Modern Forest Economy* I have stated :—

It is more easy to make intelligible the treatment so designated than it is to render in English the designation given to it. The following may be taken as supplying a rough and rude illustration of it in its application to a coppice wood. If the coppice be one which may profitably be cut down every twenty years, by dividing it into twenty equal or equivalent portions, and cutting one, but only one of these, each year, there may be obtained a constant supply of wood, the division cut in the first year being ready again for the axe in the twenty-first year of the operation, and again in the forty-first year, while the other divisions followed in their order.

This mode of exploitation has been extensively adopted in the management of coppice woods in Russia, though *Jardinage* is generally followed in the felling of timber. I have found that there on many estates held by private proprietors, there is carried out recklessly, and without system, a succession of clearings in successive years—one portion being cleared this year, another portion next year, a third portion in the year following. And on other estates, in connection with mining and smelting operations, a somewhat similar exploitation is carried out more systematically.

A similar mode of procedure has been adopted in several of the Crown forests. By Professor Sokanoff, who at the time held the Chair of Forest Economy in the Forest Corps at Lanskoi, near St. Petersburg, I was told, when there in 1873, that it was not uncommon, and it might be considered the general usage, to fell the forest in long strips of 50 fathoms, or 350 feet, in breadth, alternating with strips of the same width on which the trees were left standing to sow the cleared ground. Where wood is scarce they clear these strips completely; where it is abundant they leave young trees unfelled to grow, or be destroyed in the removal of the others, as may happen; and when a new growth of trees has been fairly established on the cleared strip, the strip of standing trees is cleared if there be a probability of its being re-sown or otherwise restocked with trees.

A similiar account was given to me of the cutting of fuel for a smelting furnace in the Government of Orenburg. Thirty years was deemed sufficient for the reproduction and growth of the firewood, and the whole was divided into thirty equivalent portions, each of which was allotted for one year's exploitation in the expectation that in thirty years it would be reproduced. Strips were the forms in which the several portions were laid out, and these, so far as was practicable, were made to converge towards the forge; and in felling each a strip was left unfelled for the production of seed for the natural re-sowing of the portion cleared. My informant stated that the strip left was either one-sixth or one-twelfth of the breadth of the strip cleared—he could not recollect which. I think it probably it was left at the side, and that those

of two contiguous ridges were contiguous, whereby they
might be conjointly one-sixth of the breadth of one cleared
strip, but one-twelfth of two if the felling did not follow
each other in due succession.

Advantages likely to follow such a method of managing
forests suggest themselves at once, and, as described, it
seems to be one which must be of easy application anywhere. But the practical forester who has given attention to my statement may have remarked that I have
used the expression *equal or equivalent* portions. Good
will result from the adoption of division into equal
portions—much good, but with a large admixture of evil.
Equal portions are not necessarily equivalent portions,
and such is the variation in the productiveness of different
portions of a forest, from variation in soil, in exposure,
and in adaptation to the growth of the kind of tree which
happens to be upon it, that it is very improbable that
many portions equal in extent will be equal in productiveness, if any at all happen to be so; and therefore the
division of a forest into equal portions will not yield
advantages equal to what would be obtained by the division of the forest into what I have called equivalent
portions.

With the attempt to do this commences the difficulties
of the undertaking. Equivalent partitions cannot be
obtained by divisions founded on equality of superficial
areas, neither can they be obtained by divisions
founded on the number of trees growing in each, or even
on the cubic contents of these. The soil, the exposure,
the kind of tree growing in different localities, the adaptation of the soil and of the exposure to the growth of the
kind of tree, or of trees, growing in each, the age or ages
of these trees, the rate of their annual increase at different
ages, the age or ages at which they respectively attain
their maximum growth, and at which they attain their
maximum of value,—these, and twenty other points, must
be determined to furnish the data necessary to determine
equivalent partitions; and such partitions are necessary

in order to ensure the full benefits of this method of forest management being secured.

If by a tentative process, based on superficial extent, as it necessarily must be, modified in accordance with the number of trees, and with the cubic contents of these, it be sought to arrive at a division of a forest into equivalent partitions, it will be found that constant modifications of the division first made are seen to be necessary. By proceeding to the work of partition with an extensive knowledge of the natural history of the trees on the ground, of the process of tree growth, and of much pertaining to meteorology, and geognosy relating thereto, the work will be found to be more easy ; but with all the forest science which has as yet been secured, the work must be to some extent tentative still ; and this is accepted as a fact by the most advanced foresters of the day.

And while this has been accepted as a fact, it has also been found that divide the forest or coppice wood as you may, you do not secure a sustained production through successive cycles of the revolution or rotation of exploitations. The second crop is not always, or indeed often, equal to the primitive or original, nor the third to the second.

It is possible ofttimes to trace in embryotic structures the rudiments of the organs of the fully developed organism ; but how different are the appearances presented by the two! How like, and yet how unlike, are the chrysalis and the butterfly! Similar is the similitude and the difference between the old system à tire et aire, and the system of forest economy now carried out in Germany and in France, and in most countries on the Continent of Europe—the most advanced forest economy of the day.

There is in this system of management a three-fold object sought, production soutenue, régéneration naturelle, and amélioration progressive ; not one or other, but all of these combined, and so combined not only that each shall

be secured without detriment to the other
shall be secured as the result of what may b
special view to the accomplishment of any,—
in view of all promoting each, what is do
each promoting all : a combination of ends
accomplishment of one, such as is ofttimes s
for example in the honeycomb, where e
space, of material, and labour, are so cc
apparently it may with equal propriety be
the same phrase, with either of these thre
as if the one end in view.

What is sought is a sustained production
period of indefinite, infinite, or perpetual du
year, every four years, every ten years, ac
case determined may be—giving an equal p
in quantity or in value, according as the ca
shall be—equal to the maximum capability
—without diminution, periodical or per
without detriment to the forest—not only s
diminution of the forest—trees as felled b
by natural reproduction from self-sown se
reproduction of the forest and the felling
that is felled tends alike to the improvemen
—so that it shall ever be rising in value
are withdrawn.

This is what is meant by sustained prodt
regeneration, and progressive amelioration (
may be said, incredulously—If forest scie
applied, can do all this, it can work won
away one's breath to read it ! Well, such
forest economy as carried out in France, a
being accomplished ; nor in France alone,
sections of the German Empire ; and it is
perfection of forest management to whicl
forest science throughout the Continent (
seeking to bring the management of forests
with which they are severally connected.

This method of exploitation has been to

introduced into Russia, where it is known as the scientific method of exploitation; in Germany it is known as *Die Fachwerke Method;* in France, as *La Methode des Compartiments.* But it has not been introduced to such an extent in this part of Russia as to call for a detail of its successive operations. Such details are given in *Introduction to the Study of Modern Forest Economy* [pp. 165-186], and more briefly in the *French Forest Ordinance of* 1669 [pp. 45-47]. In this place mention is made of it to indicate the position in the development of the method adopted of forest economy. This method of exploitation has been adopted more or less extensively, and more or less perfectly, in the Governments of Tula, Orel, Kaluga, and others in which mining operations or manufactories are extensively carried on; and these operations it has been sought to regulate by legislative enactments.

The area of forests of which concessions have been made, is understood to be 5,394,000 *decatins,* or 5,995,028 *hectares.*

Atkinson, in his work entitled *Oriental and Western Siberia,* writing of the estate of the Demidoffs, says :—

'On this vast estate of the Demidoffs, containing 3,095,700 acres, nearly equalling Yorkshire, nature has been most bountiful. Iron and copper ore appear to be inexhaustible. Platinum and gold are in the upper valleys, and malachite is found there also in enormous quantities, with porphyry and jasper of great beauty, and various coloured marbles. Their forests extend over more than 10,000 square versts, and are thickly covered with timber. These woods are under the supervision of intelligent officers, whose duty it is to cut them down in proper succession. It requires a space of eighty years to reproduce timber suitable for the use of the zavods.' And again :—

'The view of the lake looking up towards Bielaya Gora, with its islands and hilly shores, is very pretty; formerly it was thickly wooded on the north side, but the timber was cut down a few years ago for the use of the zavod. In fifty or sixty years this will again be a dense forest, and that too without planting.'

It may be so; but there has not been satisfactory reproduction of felled forests everywhere; and this has been the case notwithstanding the substitution of exploitation according to the method detailed for indiscriminate fellings.

CHAPTER VII.

THE so-called famous Forest Ordinance of 1669, which has become identified with the exploitation of forests in accordance with what is known as *La Methode à Tire et Aire*, that adopted in this district, was expected to put an end at once and for ever to all malversation, peculation, and waste in the exploitation of forests to which it was applicable; and regulations equally explicit and equally stringent were issued here for the protection of forests in the district against waste and destruction. But in the one case, as in the other, the end desired was not secured. It is not unfrequently the case that both in Church and State, arrangements which seem well adapted to secure what is desired, fail in practice to prevent the evils they were designed to meet. In different countries may be seen in the administration of the forests abuses which may remind one of the apostle's saying : ' The law is good, and the commandment holy, just, and good ; but the commandment which was ordained unto life has been found to be unto death. Illustrations may be supplied from the history of forestry in Spain, in France, in England, and at the Cape of Good Hope, if not in others also of the British Colonies. And the manipulation of laws designed for the conservation, maintenance, and economic exploitation of the forests in this region to secure a sustained supply of firewood for the smelting and manufacture of the metallic products of the mines has also been in many instances most disastrous.

I have formed a high opinion of forest officials in Russia ; and I have no reason to suspect that many, if not all, of the present forest officials are not in moral character, as well as in professional skill and professional knowledge, such as the high-minded and thoroughly educated gentlemen of the service with whom I have been brought into personal communication and correspondence. But once it was otherwise, and it may be long before either the physical or the moral effects of long-continued abuse of forests and long-continued abuse of official powers are altogether eradicated.

Mining proprietors of forests can do with their forest products as they chose, so long as these had not in some way or another come under the surveillance of the Government. It is of State forests only that I write, and I write of what has occurred in times past, though times not very remote from the present.

It has been the case, if it be not so still, that underlying the question of remuneration of officials in the service of Government is the idea that it is an honour to a man to serve his country, and that such service is best recompensed by honour; and personal rank supplemented with orders of knighthood, with appropriate decorations, are the rewards dispensed with liberal hand by the Government in almost all departments of the service, but often without adequate pecuniary pay to cover necessary personal and family expenditure.

In answer to enquires, one of my correspondents in this district wrote to me:—

'I was well acquainted with the *Glavnoi Laesnicki*, or Commissioner of Woods and Forests in the district in which are situated the mining works of the Ural. He told me his range extended over thousands of versts in the Governments of Nijni Novgorod, Kazan, Viatka, Perm, Tobolsk, Orenburg, and Ufa, and he received the large salary of 800 roubles !—less than £100 a year. He had under-foresters in each district and at Government works, all paid upon a like scale ! and these again had woodmen to look after the felling and delivery of the timber, and there was beside a cordon of guards all around at all points, and on every road.' Such was the staff, but what of the discharge of their duties?

These men entered the service not for the honour of the service, but as a means of livelihood ; and the custom at one time was for officials to pay themselves as much as they could by practices which every right minded person must condemn, but to which no dishonour attached there and then. I was told in the time of Nicholas that, excepting himself, there was not a man in the Empire who was not open to a bribe. The statement was, I believe, too sweeping ; but it indicated the general belief and the general practice. It was customary at that time for Government officials to wear, between two button holes on the breast of the coat, a coloured ribbon with Roman numerals in gold representing the length of time they had been in the service. And I was told of one of our countrymen, whom I knew, being wont to point to his ribbon with a knowing wink, and saying : ' Look, 14 years without ever having been detected !'

It is told of Nicholas that at a meeting of council during the Crimean war—I presume a council of war—as one proof of malversation after another connected with the manipulation of military returns, and the purchase of provisions and munitions, breaking out in passion before the generals, the nobles, and the princes at the board, and taking his son and successor by the hand, he said : ' Alexander, there is not a man in the Empire in whom I can trust but you.'

I adduce this as an indication of a moral tone which was widely prevalent, and I consider that I do no wrong to those who were then in the forest service in alleging that it is not improbable that so it was with them. If so, opportunities were not alacking for their doing as did others.

I was informed that at the time the information was given to me, by general, if not universal usage, each zavod was entitled to 300 cubic fathoms of wood a year from Government forests for the production of steam in aid of

water motive power, and a regular permit for the cutting
of this was yearly given, but much more was used, and
sometimes by appropriate manipulation more than three
times that quantity might be obtained on the same
permit. If the permit were sent to the forest inspector,
unaccompanied by a private communication, it might be
courteously received, attested, and returned with directions as to the localities in the forests whence the supply
was to be obtained; but it might be found that these
were situated some 60 or 80 versts (40 or well nigh 60
miles) from the works; in which case the expense of
transport would be more by far than the current price of
wood delivered at the zavod. But I was informed on
credible authority that if, as provision against such an
occurrence, there were handed to the inspector, along with
the permit, a sum of money enclosed in an envelope, much
more satisfactory arrangements might be made. And if
the amount enclosed amounted to 200 roubles, or £20,
arrangements might be made for the wood being cut in
forests within a tenth of that distance; but then all the
officials who were under the inspector must also be silenced
by hush money, as otherwise some fatal objection might be
raised. The forest guard might be satisfied with 20 or 30
kopecs—about 6d—but his superiors must receive much
more, according to their rank; and then though 1000 cubic
feet might be felled and delivered, in the official records
everything would be found in order—300 cubic feet
granted, 300 cubic feet felled, 300 cubic feet delivered—
the exact amount and nothing more.

But sometimes it happened that ere the delivery was
made the staff of the officials was changed, and then all
that had been done went for nothing; and the whole process of administering hush money had to be gone through
again. If this were not done with every man amongst
them, they would be found every man of them, or some
one of them at least, the very paragon of just, upright,
incorruptible officials !

But even such a case as this might be met. An instance

was reported to me, of which the following is the outline :
Wood was being felled by a contractor for the work, acting
on a permit which had been properly attested, and was
otherwise in order.   But a great deal more had been felled
than was covered by the permit, and an official went to
him saying, ' Ivan, Ivanowitch (John, the son of John)
what is this?   Look here !   There's something wrong ;
the permit is for 300 cubic feet : you have felled trees
enough to measure 1000.   You had no right to do so ; all
this must be confiscated.'   And confiscated it was ; and the
Government mark was put upon it ; after which, to dispose
of it, would make whoever did so liable to banishment to
Siberia.   But the official by whom this was done went to
the proprietor of the zavod, on whose permit it was being
felled, and said to him, ' I find the contractor has far
exceeded the quantity mentioned in the permit, and of
the excess 700 fathoms have been confiscated.   According
to the law this must be sold by public auction, but I will
sell it to you for the amount of Government dues which
must be paid upon it, the amount of which is 100 roubles.'
On these terms the wood was purchased ; the owner of the
zavod got 700 fathoms of wood for 100 roubles (£10), but
the contractor got nothing for the work he had done ; and
it is supposed that in such a case the Government would
never see a kopec of the payment made.   Things were
thus made pleasant to all, excepting to the contractor, who
had to grin and bear the loss, hoping that things would go
better with him next time.

A case was reported to me of a contractor for felling
wood who, either by way of making up a loss sustained in
some such way, or more likely in the ordinary execution
of his work, having delivered the quantity of wood specified in the permit—or it may be some larger quantity which
this was made to cover—and having received payment for
this according to agreement, he altered the date of the
permit, and proceeded to fell more wood, with this as
his sanction, the following year.   All went on without

interruption till the work was completed, and he was
about to deliver the wood felled, when one of the officials,
through whose hands the paper had to pass, coming to
him with the usual question, ' Ivan, Ivanowitch, what is
this ?' said to him, ' This is an old permit which has already
passed through our office ; the date has been altered by some
one ; I am sorry for you, but all this wood must be confiscated.'   Both parties knew well who was in fault; the
man had to submit, shrugged his shoulders it may be, and
expressed his thanks that the official had not pressed
the matter further, and brought against him a criminal
charge.   But he sent an account of the whole matter
to his brother, who was resident in the Government town.
He waited upon the Governor and informed him that his
brother had become involved in a very unpleasant business,
but one which could be satisfactorily explained, notwithstanding that appearances were much against him ; and he
gave his explanation of the matter, upon hearing which the
Governor said, ' All right ! It is an unfortunate occurrence ; but we can get it rectified.'   The brother thanked
him, and left.   In the evening he called again on the
Governor at the Residence.   After having had a cup of
tea, they sat down to play a game at cards ; and before
they rose he managed to lose a large sum to the Governor
—the amount reported to me was 8000 roubles—and he
went away a happy man.   Next day, on calling at the
chancellory or office, he found everything had been
arranged !   It had been discovered that it was altogether
a mistake—the supposed alteration of the date of the
permit ; and the wood which had been felled was restored
to the contractor.

So much for the case having been brought before a
Governor who, in a long tenure of office, *was never known
to have accepted a bribe !*   The name of the Government
was supplied to me.

I was told of other Governors who had a like reputation,
and who, had a bribe been offered to them, would have

been indignant and resented the insult given to them, as would any gentleman whatever his nation. But with such I was told, and I speak only of what was reported to me of proceedings in the district, and commanded my belief as substantially true, that in such a case the business must be conducted with greater delicacy; and my informant, apparently having some case—and more than that one case—in his eye, said, so far as I can reproduce his statement: ' In any difficulty, a diamond ornament, or if the matter will warrant the greater expense, a whole set of diamond ornaments may be presented to the wife of the Governor ; and in subsequent conversation, it may be days afterwards, she must be made acquainted with the irregularity which has occurred and been discovered. The Scots have a proverb to the effect ' that a wink is as good as a nod to a blind horse;' and the Romans had a saying, quoted sometimes in our day, in the abbreviated form, *verbum sap.* On that day or the next, or otherwise on some befitting opportunity, she guilelessly inquires of her liege lord, addressing him with the usual designation expressive of endearment : ' *Dooshinka*, what is that story about So-and-So ?' 'It is so-and-so,' is the reply; which is followed by the rejoinder, ' I am sorry for that—he is such a nice man—a good man he is. Can you not help him in his difficulties? I wish you could. If you can will you do so? Do so for my sake. Perhaps he was wrong; but he is a nice man; perhaps it was all a mistake.' ' No, no; nothing can be done.' 'Oh ! *Dooshinka*, try if you can help him. I know him to be an honest man.' ' Very well, *Goloobchick*, I shall look into the case to-morrow, and if I find that he is not to blame I shall see what can be done in the matter.' ' I thank you, *Dooshinka;* it is so like you.' And the result in all probability is that it is discovered the charge against the donor of the diamonds was founded altogether on a mistake—and a mistake which can easily be rectified !

The picture is a sad one, but it is only in accordance with what is notorious in Russia, and universally believed ;

K

in accordance with what has come under my own observation; in accordance with what has come within the
experience of my personal friends, both fifty years ago and
in later times; in accordance with stories innumerable,
current in conversation and reproduced in tales; and
assuming that they may be only founded on fact, and not
literally true, the student of forest science with the knowledge of like malversations which have occurred in France
and England, and of the waste and destruction of forests
which have thence resulted, will not be surprised if he be
told that in such circumstances there has been great devas-
tation of forests. He will probably coolly remark—I could
have foretold what the issue would be !

Like malversation I found presenting other phases. Restrictions put upon the consumption of wood as fuel
employed in the production of steam-power were thus
evaded.   There were similar restrictions put upon the
extravagant consumption of fuel in domestic life; and
residents there have like stories to tell of ways in which
these are evaded.
    One of my correspondents, in the correctness of whose
statements I have confidence, wrote to me : ' The quantity
of firewood to be allowed for heating and cooking seems
to have been left to the discretion of the Chief Commissioner of the Imperial Forests ; and you have to address and
present to him a petition for authorative permission to
cut down the quantity allowed to you—he having a list
of those persons who have had this privilege granted to
them.   Moreover, you have to state in your petition how
many houses, rooms, and fire-grates you have requiring
fuel : he is already provided with a list, not only of
yours, but of every dwelling in his district; and there
is a certain quantity told off as at your disposal.   I forget
what it is, but amply sufficient—in fact, there are few that
take all they might, and this gives them a margin to work
upon, as I shall by-and-by explain.   All this seems
fair, and above board ; and so it would be if it were fairly

carried out; but there come in mutual operations of the
legally right and morally wrong principle which is so prevalent in Russia, which I have referred to before.   When
your petition is presented, if it be unaccompanied by something to make it presentable, it will be a long time before
it is answered, and you may long dance attendance before
there is time to attend to you.   There is such an awful
press of business—so many to be attended to before your
turn comes! The proper authorities are not at home, gone
to other districts, cannot tell when will be best; and
when it does come your quittance is numbered for the most
distant estate in the boundary of your town, perhaps 40 or
60 versts off, instead of 8 or 12, and what are you to do?
What can you do?   The thing is legally right, and that
brings up the price of your firewood a rouble, or 1·50
roubles a sajen or more, if you can get it cut at all. But to
whom can you complain? And what have you to complain
of? But take personally—you cannot send—a good round
douceur in proportion to the quantity required, say about
a fourth of what it would otherwise cost you, and you will
bring back the order with you for the Under Forest Commissioner to allow you to commence operations at once on
the estate under his care—but it does not say where, so
you have not done yet.   There is more oil to be made use
of; it is a long time before the machinery moves, and
when it does, the wood is not of the kind and in the place
you want, and only the money leverage will remove that
obstacle.   But you have not done yet.   There are all the
under strappers, whose eyes have got to be bandaged, and
whose mouths have got to be stopped with paper roubles.
And you have not done yet; you have now to give the order
into the hands of a wood-cutter, and you make another
agreement with him for delivery on your grounds of the
quantity specified at so much per sajen, hard money
down; but it is an understood thing by all parties that the
operation will not be strictly looked after, that is, when
all parties are satisfied, so you get double or triple the
quantity of wood you have paid dues for. That is, if your

wood-cutter does not turn out a bigger rascal than all the rest, and fail to carry out your verbal agreement, or goes and sells your wood to some one else; and you are always at his mercy, as he always has his money beforehand, otherwise he won't undertake the work.

'Perhaps you will say, Why be drawn into this corrupt and disreputable way of doing business? There is no other way of obtaining timber, and you must either do in Rome as the Romans do in these matters, or shut up shop and clear out altogether. There is indeed another way, worse still, which many follow, and have to do so, who have no right to timber. There are a gang of men called forest robbers, or wood stealers; they will supply you with a limited quantity at their own risk till they get it on your premises in the night time; but as it is without the Government stamp, which all timber ought to have before it is allowed to pass the sentinels who should be on the watch night and day on every road leading out of the forests, you have got to account to the authorities as to how it came into your possession without permission, if it be discovered there; when nothing releases you from criminal prosecution except paying black mail again.

'You must know that each town, and village, and zavod there on the Ural, has forests for the sole use of the peasantry, for the building of their houses, the heating of their dwellings, &c., and these forests are under the care of the town authorities and the village communes, and the head of each family is apportioned off a lot as it is decided upon at their meetings. I can relate you another anecdote illustrative of this. There is a party who had his papers all in order, and had the right to his yearly quantum of timber and firewood. There came a wood-cutter to him, who said he had timbers to dispose of that were legally his, cut down from their own woods to build himself a house with; but that he could not go on with this. Well, the bargain is struck, and the timber is delivered; but it turns out to be fresh cut, and without the necessary brand!

'The next day there appeared at the mill a police official, and a town councillor. The manager happened to be outside, and demanded to know their business. They said, "You have stolen timbers on your premises, cut down from the town forest just at hand. We have seen the place, and we are come to confiscate them, and make out a criminal protocol against you." "Very well, gentlemen," says the Englishman, " show me your warrant and authority for searching my premises before you proceed any further." They had reckoned without their host, and had nothing to show but the uniform of one of them, while the other had a book of laws in his hand. The Englishman says, " I don't know you; I can't receive you without the legal authorised document." They went away in a great rage, vowing dreadful things. The Englishman saw he was likely to get into a mess, and that there was no time to be lost, so he went immediately to the under Government forester, and told him all the case. " Oh," says he, " make yourself easy." A man was sent off by post-horses, 30 versts for his stamp. And when the gentlemen returned next morning with redoubled force, and all the necessary legal forms, every timber and block on the premises had got the Government brand, his papers were all in order, Government was paid, and there were timbers yet to receive. They retired crest-fallen, but laughed heartily at the ruse ; they saw through the whole affair, but it was legally right, so they gave the Englishman the credit of being a shrewd fellow, beating them at their own game; and he, instead of prosecuting for damages for a false charge, wined and dined them, and they left him in peace ever afterwards. He had every reason to believe that the very rascal that brought him the timber went and informed upon him.

'Well, now, I think you will see from what I have written that it is no wonder the forests are rapidly disappearing in all parts of Russia, especially when we consider the careless humble-jumble "self first" system of theirs, and besides this, the want of a proper scientific

the contents of so bulky a letter may have been,
may have led to its being opened; and the case is
adduced to show that there was nothing out of keeping
with the practice of the country in the malversations and
abuses in the forest service which I have cited.

It may be supposed that there is now some security
against wrongs in trial by jury, which has been introduced
into Russia; but on my saying this to a practical man, long
conversant with the management of works in the district,
and with doings such as I have reported, his reply was: —
'It may seem so to you ; and the rule of Court regulating
procedure may seem to be all that could be desired to
secure justice being done; but the judge can be bribed
as efficiently as this could be done in the days of Nicholas;
and if you can secure the judge, you can secure your case.
And I'll tell you how it is done.' Naming then a successful practitioner in Jury Courts, he said:—'Here is an important case ; and he will have nothing to do with any others.
His terms are that his client shall pay all expenses
incurred in preparing papers required in the prosecution
of the case, and pay him say 20,000 roubles if he gain the
case, but only 5000 roubles if he happen to fail to do so.
This being securely arranged, one half of the 20,000
roubles is by the practitioner given to the judge. He then
enters the court, assured that the case is prejudged in his
favour ; and he finds that such a charge is given to the jury
that it is morally impossible that they can give a verdict
other than that for which he has paid.

As with the Jury Court, so with the village Court. One of
my informants in regard to forest operations on the Urals,
referring to what had been the experience of another in
regard to punishments which were sometimes inflicted,
said to me :—'I have no doubt of the correctness of what is
stated, in so far as it relates to what was witnessed and
heard by your friend at that time ; but it is not in accordance with my experience. The rod employed is composed
of birch twigs, bound firmly together in a bundle sometimes three inches thick. The knout has been abolished ;

and so has punishment with the lash, which consisted of three thongs; but punishment with birch rods is still legal, and the village magistrates have authority to order punishment with them to the extent of 25 strokes.'

He added :—' In connection with my work in the forest I frequently had occasion formally to lodge complaints with the authorities against men in my employment getting drunk, or otherwise leaving or neglecting their work, and such was the punishment awarded for such offences ; but it was of no avail, and I was pestered with my workmen. One day a centurion, placed over a hundred men, quietly said to me, "I do not know how you do it ; you send in your complaint; and they only laugh at you for your complaints. The usage here is to send with your complaint a three rouble note. Do this the next time, and you will see the difference." ' He did so, when to his horror four soldiers were sent for; the accused was laid on his belly, with a small pillow for his head ; one soldier took his seat upon his neck, another on his feet, his back was bared, and the other two soldiers, one on each side, inflicted the stripes according to the sentence, every one of them drawing blood. The raw wound was then rubbed with salt, and the man was left to do as he choose until he might be again fit for work.

My informant was horrified ; but never again had he occasion to make complaint of his men. It is as likely as not that it was at the instance of those who benefited by the *douceur* that my informant was told of the national usage in regard to a gift.

So much for bribery in courts of justice, which is referred to in passing as an indication of the universality of the practice.

Returning to bribery practised in the field, I may state that the grant of wood to proprietors of extensive works is made to enable them to supplement water-power by steam, or to make use of this exclusively. No steam-engine may be used in Russia until it is certified by a

Government engineer that it has been examined by him and found satisfactory. The law applies to railway locomotives, steamboats, and stationary engines alike. An engineer employed in the construction of such engines gave to me details of one case which occurred in connection with an engine which he erected, and told me it was illustrative of what is of frequent, if not of constant occurrence.

The engine was erected; he sent a specification of its power, &c., to the inspector, and along with this the usual gratuity; the gratuity was a large one, and in due course there came a certificate that the engine had been examined, and everything found to be in accordance with the specifications. But it was requisite that the certificate of approval should bear the certification of three officials connected with the police, that they had been present when the inspection was made. The two papers, the specification and the certificate of the inspector, were next sent to the police office, and along with them a comparatively trifling gratuity. And these were in due course returned duly attested, signed, and sealed, though neither inspector nor police officials had ever seen the engine in question, or gone to see it. And had the boiler, within a week or less, exploded, destroying life and property to any extent, that certificate would have protected the constructing engineer from all penal consequences.*

---

* Some one on reading this may feel prompted to say, 'Thank God we have no such rascality in Britain.' If it be so, give God the thanks—but is it so? Since my return from Russia I have read the following in a Scottish newspaper :—'The article above recalls something that happened ten years ago in an old-fashioned town in Fife, where I was visiting. Having called on my friend, I found him engaged, so I said I would just take a walk to the bay, and see what was doing at the building yard. On passing it I observed a large steamer on the stocks, and all but ready for the painter. As she looked a fine craft, I walked up the plank, or gangway, and got on deck. It happened to be the dinner hour, and there were only one or two 'prentice boys walking about. I first stepped to the stern, examining all very carefully, then passed the 'prentice, while walking forward to the bow. On passing I called his attention to the sides of two rivet-holes, where there were two cracks fully two inches in length. Young as the boy was, he knew what he was after, and in answering me, he said, such holes or cracks could not be helped, on account of the iron plates being so bad, and they were caused in punching them, as it was far too expensive to bore them. I asked, "Is the bottom of the ship built of the same material?" to which he said, "Yes, and some *not so good;* but when it is puttied and painted it is never seen!" However, I said nothing. After I had left him I saw him running on shore, but I just thought he was hurrying off to his dinner. However, in ten minutes I saw the shipbuilder himself coming

The following is another illustration of the corrupt practices prevalent extensively, which, though not apparently pertaining to forestry, is indirectly connected with the forest lands of the district : There are in the Ural mountains mines of valuable marble. Of this much is hewn on the spot, not only into blocks for transport but into articles of ornament and luxury in Government works. These products are despatched to the capital, under charge of a subaltern commissioned officer, known for the time as the captain of the caravan. An officer of high rank, the father of the bride of the son of my informant, gave to my informant the following account of his early experience and initiation into the mysteries of jobbery. He was favoured with an appointment to the office of captain of the caravan while he was still but a youthful officer. He attended to the charge with commendable care, but in despite of this some little injuries were sustained by the works of art under his charge. These he got repaired at a very moderate charge indeed, and he went with elated spirits to lodge his accounts with the head of the department in the capital. Never had the transport been managed so efficiently

hurriedly from his office, and behind him his son ; so I just left the vessel to meet him, as I knew them both. In his hurry he passed me, and remarked, "There is a gentleman on board whom I wish to see ; please excuse me at present ;" so he passed on. On coming up to his son, I remarked, "Your father is in a hurry ; is there anything wrong, as he scarcely stopped to speak?" He answered, "Oh, yes ! he expects to find a gentleman on board, an inspector we were expecting next week. But he has rather taken us by surprise." I said, "How could he do that?" He answered, "There are certain things to be done before he sees the ship, and he may find fault at this time." In my mind I thought it was rather strange, so I began to ask him where he got the iron he built the ship with. He told me the name. I said, "Was that the best place to get good iron ?" He answered, "No. But, you see, when we are tied to a price we cannot afford to put in so good iron." I said to him, "Is that inferior iron capable of being punched without the iron cracking ?" He said, "No. All, or most every plate, is more or less cracked." I said, "If you bored the plates would they not be better ?" He said, "Yes ; but it's too expensive." Just then his father returned, and remarked what an alarm he had got, as the boy had run to the office and said a man was examining the ship, and finding fault with the iron and cracked bolt holes. This ship, I learned some months after, had left and never was heard of again after sailing—supposed to have foundered ; and how could it be otherwise ? The vessel straining would put out the putty, and then the water would come in and sink her. After that I learned three other vessels, built by the same man, never reached their first voyage, and in one was his own son and nephew. I also learned no inspector ever saw the ships till puttied and painted. This is how many valuable lives are lost, and the insurance companies punished. One of the ships, 300 tons, was supposed to capsize—having iron masts far too heavy for her to carry without canvas.' If such things be done in Scotland need we wonder at anything I have reported should have been done in Russia, one is reminded of the mote and the beam.

and economically; but this called forth, beyond the mention of the fact, no commendation from the officer to whom the accounts were delivered, who simply courteously desired him to call next day. He did so, and was then desired to see the head of the department in his room. He went, anticipating a full meed of praise, but he was confounded with a surly question, 'Are these your accounts, sir; and how have you dared to spend, or to say you have spent, Imperial funds without due authority?' All explanations were in vain, calling forth fresh outbursts of passion. He was kept for weeks making bootless calls at the office, increasing what was to him a very inconvenient expense living in the capital. But there was no appearance of any progress being made in getting his accounts passed; and until these were passed he could not leave. At length one of the officials pitying him, taking him aside asked, 'What is the amount in dispute?' 'One hundred and twenty roubles (£12) for repairs for injuries sustained by the goods in transit.'

'This is apparently the first time you have come in charge of the caravan?' 'It is,' was the reply.

'Then you must ask permission to give in a corrected statement of your outlay; and I will aid you in the preparation of this.' The application was made; and the permission was granted.

'Now,' said his informant, 'You must state the whole outlay on the journey, and this very differently. You must increase the charge under every head a hundredfold, and add under each charge as a separate item "incidental expenses" to a corresponding account.' It is the old story of the unjust steward. 'How much owest thou?— an hundred measures of oil.' 'Take thy bill and sit down quickly, and write fifty.' . . 'And how much owest thou?' And he said, 'an hundred measures of wheat.' And he said unto him, 'Take thy bill and write fourscore'

But here, the case being different, the process is reversed; and by this means 5000 roubles were added to the account. 'Now,' said the adviser, 'that will do.' The young officer presented the corrected account. He was told to come again the next day. Again he was told you must see the chief of the department.

He went to his room with fear and trembling; he was received as if the accounts were being presented for the first time. He was complimented on the zeal and care with which he had discharged the duty entrusted to him, and on the very reasonable amount of the expenses which had been incurred. But whether all this was said in irony or otherwise he knew not. He was told to call next day at the office. He did so, fearing he had fallen into a trap, but was at once informed that his accounts were passed, and presented with authority to draw the amount. He drew it accordingly; but following instructions received from his adviser, he waited upon the head of the department to take leave, and handed to him a closed envelope containing the surcharge of 5000 roubles. This was received in apparent ignorance of its contents, but he was asked to call once more before he set off on his return journey. He did so, and received from the head of the department, with the parting *Gluckliche Reise*, a closed envelope. Upon afterwards opening this he found that it contained 500 roubles, his share of the spoil. 'Such,' said the officer of rank, ' was my initiation into the mysteries of the service.'

The reader would err who should conclude that the Ural mining district must be, in comparison with other parts of Russia, a sink of iniquity, and all connected with the operations carried on there greater sinners than all the sinners in the land. It is not so. I had almost said it is the same everywhere. I only hesitated because I could not prove so sweeping an assertion. I may say, however, that according to all accounts the facts reported are, taking in accordance with the customs of the country, only their special form from the conditions and usages of the locality. In so far as Government officials in the forest service have conformed to these they have only done as governors, judges, military authorities, and officials in all departments of the service may have done.

In all these positions there are men of high moral worth, and there are, personally known to me, forest officials of high position in the service, and others in subordinate positions in the forest service of Russia, who are men of noble mind and high principle, who would condemn such proceedings as indignantly as may any one of my readers, and who, I doubt not, would say, ' If such things be, by all means let it be known ; truth, like light, makes all things manifest; it is by an improved scientific conservation, exploitation, and extension of our forests that we hope to preserve for our country an ample supply of timber and of firewood for years to come, and if in all our endeavours we are handicapped thus, the sooner we and others know it the better.' Not only are there such known to me, but I have never happened to make the acquaintance or meet with one of a different spirit. I do not the less, however, believe that things are, or have been, as they have been represented to me in the mining districts of the Ural mountains.

And I hold it to be desirable that the student of forest science in other lands should know not a little of the multiform evils against which the practical forest administrator has ofttimes to contend. All that has been stated I can cap with statements of like nefarious proceedings in France, previous to the enactment of the famous Forest Ordinance of 1669, and with like proceedings in England within the last half century ; while the case of engineers certifying the efficiency of steam-engines they had never seen, is, I consider, equalled by what I have shown is reported to have occurred in Scotland within the last ten years.

But what I have more especially in view is to report the conditions under which the now antiquated method of exploitation known as *La Methode à Tire et Aire* is being carried out here, that students of forest science in judging this may distinguish things which differ, and while accepting proof of its inherent defects, not over-estimate these by confounding with them abuses for which it is not responsible.

CHAPTER VIII.

CONDITIONS OCCASIONING A DIMINISHED SUPPLY
OF WOOD.

IN view of what has been stated in the immediately preceding chapters, little surprise need be felt that through a
lack of sufficient wood for fuel, consequent on an impoverishment of the forests, the industrial operations
peculiar to the district should be in a state of depression.
The method of forest exploitation followed—that known as
La Methode à Tire et Aire—like that of *Jardinage*, practised
in the northern Governments of Olonetz, Archangel, and
Vologda, is in itself radically defective as a means of
securing from forests a sustained supply of produce.

When in France and in Germany it was carried out in
strict accordance with the principle upon which it was
based, even then it failed to secure a sustained supply of
wood. Here it is not carried out under its normal conditions ; and there have been malversations and abuses which
have expedited the destruction or impoverishment of the
forests. In the *Forest Code* are given, properly codified in
a distinct chapter, the regulations, which have been issued,
and are supposed to be still in force, to prevent waste ; but,
as has been seen, there are devices by which any regulations may have been evaded.

The prescriptions of the *Forest Code*, relative to forests
supplying fuel for smelting and manufacturing operations
in the Ural district, are codified under Nos. 1236-1287 of
the *Ustaff Laesnoi*.

Successive chapters in this book embody the general
laws in relation to such forests; those relating to Govern-

ment forests attached to Government mines, and to private industrial undertakings in the Ural mountains; to Government forests assigned to the mining works of Altai and Nerchinsk; to forests enrolled as belonging to Government distilleries in the Government of Viatka; to forests providing supplies to the Government small arms manufactory at Tula; to Government forests enrolled as belonging to salt works, Imperial and private.

The codified forest laws relative to Government forests attached to Government mines and private industrial undertakings in the Ural districts, embody in successive sections those relating to descriptions of forests attached to such works; to the measurement of such; to the allotment of forests to such works; to the mode of surveying the actual contents of such forests and other allotments assigned to such works; to the felling of timber in these; to the allotment of timber or firewood to the inhabitants of forests which have been assigned to the Government mines; and the preservation of forests from fire.

In the appendix are laid down numerous instructions in regard to the management of these, embracing, amongst others, instructions relative to the surveying and charting, and the conservation and management, embracing both general directions and special; to the natural renovation of the woods by felling in accordance with the principles of forest science; to the order and mode of exploitation; the extent of sections; the period of revolution, fixed at 100 years; to artificial plantations by sowing—by planting on hills; and by planting on level ground; to the management of nurseries—with special regulations applicable to various subjects, and requiring information to be supplied in regular reports with requisite charts, &c., and within a limited time after the execution of all such proceedings.

In the Ural mountains I was informed that there are 69,800,000 decatins of forest land, of which 44,914,000 are woods, or 58 per cent. of the whole. I give the information as I received it, but I do so with a feeling that there must be some misapprehension, but what it is I know not.

L

I have spoken of the method of exploitation followed as
being inherently defective as a means of securing a sustained supply of produce from a forest.

In a preceding chapter I have referred to modifications
of it which have been adopted with advantage under other
designations in other parts of Russia and elsewhere. And
the necessity for this speaks of some defect of it in its
normal condition. But here the method has not, through
malversation and abuses, had fair play; it has not been
carried out in its entirety, and in accordance with the
principles upon which it was based.

It may seem to be a truism to say that if more be taken
from a forest in any specified time—a year, a decade, or a
century—than is produced in it by growth or vegetation
in the same period, the forest will be impoverished, and will
ultimately perish, though if no more be taken from it than
is produced it may continue to flourish and bring forth
abundantly. Thus, apparently, is it here. I say apparently, because, while I have learned enough to justify me
in concluding that it is so, I have not learned so much as
to warrant me, fearless of contradiction, to allege that such
is actually the case.

It is the case that the actual condition of the forests,
compared with what is reported to have been their condition previous to the introduction and development of the
local industry, is itself evidence that more has been taken
from the forests than the equivalent of what has been
produced within the time during which this has been
done. But more is required. I have already attributed
this in part to abuses and malversations. It would be
difficult, without additional information, to demonstrate
that these are the causes of which this is the effect, but with
such abuses and malversations going on as those which I
have narrated, and of which I have been credibly informed,
it seems to be natural and not unjust to conclude that
they are one cause of the disappearance of forests within
so short a period. But while they may be one cause of

this, it does not follow that they are the only cause or occasion of this. The question with which we have now to do is one relative to the merits and demerits of this method of exploiting forests, seen in the light of the facts which I have stated. Officials in the forest service of Russia are dealing manfully with existing evils. With a view to the instruction of aliens, my countrymen and others, I have stated my opinion that a method of exploitation inherently defective has here become still more manifestly defective through conditions under which it has been practised. It is, moreover, my opinion that the appropriate remedy in any similar case would be that which is being adopted—an endeavour to supersede this by an improved exploitation in accordance with the principles regulating the improve· ment which has been carried out successfully elsewhere.

The Ordinance of 1669, published in France, which is associated with this method of exploitation, is still spoken of as the famous Forest Ordinance of 1669. The principle upon which it was based was extensively adopted, not only in France, but also elsewhere. Less than 150 years, however, sufficed to show that it was not in its original form a panacea for the evils in connection with forest exploitation which were everywhere in Central Europe being deprecated. It was found that the reproduced crop did not equal in cubic contents the crop which had been cleared away. And early in the present century there was devised, primarily and chiefly by Hartig and Cotta, a modification of the method which seems to meet every desideratum, and which, so far as I know, excepting in this Government and the regions around, it has superseded that method of exploitation from which some 200 years ago so much was expected. It is known in different countries as *Die Fachwerke Method*, or *La Methode des Compartiments*, or *the Scientific* method of exploitation.

In this the forest, or a number of forests associated together, are divided into sections corresponding to the

number of decades in the age at which the trees are to be
felled; these sections are subdivided into lots, and the
required supply of wood is obtained from the clearing of
specified lots, and the first, second, or third of successive thinnings to which other specified lots are subjected—
with the result that there is secured simultaneously an
improved condition of the forest—a sustained production
of firewood or timber—and a natural reproduction of the
forest from self-sown seed.

The success which has accompanied the exploitation of
some forests here, in accordance with the now antiquated
and superseded method known as à *tire et aire*, I consider
to be attributable to one or more—probably in part to
each—of the following conditions under which it has been
practised :—

1. An efficient and sufficent protection of the forests
against waste and theft ;

2. Most of the reproduced wood being the produce of
fresh growth from old stumps, and only a small portion
of it the produce of the growth of seedlings ; and

3. The annual demand not being in excess of the annual
production of wood.

While I thus classify the conditions under which I consider that the results have been obtained, I know that the
classification is open to the objections—first, that what has
been stated last covers what goes before, and a great deal
besides ; and secondly, that it is virtually a truism or
restatement of the case in altered phraseology. But it is
nevertheless the case that elsewhere waste and theft have
helped to prevent like success being obtained ; that a cycle
appropriate to trees which send out shoots from stumps
may be sufficient to secure reproduction, while a similar
cycle would be insufficient to secure full reproduction of
the same or other kinds of trees from seed. And it is
probable that in many cases in which this method of
exploitation failed it might have proved efficient if a more
lengthened period had been allowed for reproduction.

Cases have come under my notice in which the revolution or cycle had been determined thus : a year's supply of fuel would clear a certain area of forest ; the entire forest contains a hundred times that area ; it is divided into ten sections, and a decade is assigned to the exploitation of each section. The only factors here are the requirement and the area, without regard to the annual or centennial production of wood, which should have been treated as the most important factor of the three. In consequence of this all may go well for a hundred years ; but it will be otherwise in the hundred years which follow these ; and again in the hundred years which follow them.

It would have been more reasonable to have ascertained what was the measurement of the annual or centenial production of wood, and to have divided the area in accordance with this produce instead of in accordance with the demand. Nor is it any objection to this that in that case the work for which the fuel is required must be limited accordingly. The limitation must come sooner or later, and it is bad economy to kill the goose that lays the golden egg.

A like principle is applicable to forests yielding timber ; but it is in connection with forests yielding fuel that the subject comes under consideration here. And in connection with this it falls to be mentioned that the determination of the measurement of wood produced in a year, a decade, or a century, is more complicated than may at first be supposed.

The relative increase in cubic measurement varies in a tree at different ages. It does so to such an extent that in trees which grow vigorously to the age of 150 years more wood may be obtained in the course of 300 years from three fellings, a hundred years apart, than from two fellings 150 years apart. And in coppice, possibly more wood may be obtained in 300 years by felling once in forty years than by felling only once in sixty years. The age at which trees should be felled with a view to procure from them the maximum of produce, whether of timber or of firewool, is a point to which the scientific forester finds it necessary in many cases to give special attention; and this is not the same for all kinds of trees, nor for all forests of the same kind of trees, varying as these do in soil and latitude and exposure.

In the case of two woods or forests in the Government of Ufa we have it stated:—

'5. After a lapse of forty years the cleared forest is again fit for felling. In the cleared sections the forest grows thicker than it was before. . . . .

'10. The young growth grows more than double as compared with the old wood that is cut.'

Much more explicit information than this would be required to enable a scientific forester to give a scientific deliverance on several questions, all of them of essential importance to a satisfactory determination of the best treatment to which such forests should be subjected in accordance with the most advanced forest science of the day; but apparently in the opinion of those who are engaged in the management of these forests, when they are felled in a cycle of forty years more wood is produced by young woods on ground which had been cleared, than was produced there by the virgin forest.

The fact may be apparently inconsistent with the gradual diminution of woods and forests in France and in other countries on the Continent of Europe during a century and a-half, and more, that this mode of exploitation was followed there; and with the diminution of woods, and continuous rise in the price of wood required as fuel in the metallurgical works in the Ural and other districts in which this mode of exploitation has been followed. Apparently inconsistent it may be; but it is not necessarily incompatible with these other facts.

It remains to be seen whether the increased productiveness will be sustained in a second and a third crop; I anticipate that it will not. But be this as it may—a cycle of the same duration—forty years—will not necessarily be equally adapted to other kinds of trees, or to the same kinds of trees grown under different conditions. Any cycle determined solely by the produce required for metallurgical operations may prove too brief for the trees to yield the quantity of timber required; and had the cycle in this case been one of twenty-five years, instead of one of forty years, the result might have been different.

CHAPTER IX.

PARTING GLIMPSES OF LIFE IN THE DISTRICT.

REMOTE as once Siberia seemed, and was with the time required to journey thither viewed as the measurement, it is no longer to the traveller by steam a land that is afar off. 'We quitted Kazan,' writes Dr Lansdell, 'on Monday morning in one of Lubinoff's steamers, and, after proceeding two or three hours down the Volga, left that river to finish its career of 2,200 miles, whilst we turned into one of its affluents, the Kama, which is no mean river in itself, having a course of 1,400 miles. The junction of the two streams presents a fine expanse of water, but the banks are too flat to be pretty. Steamboat travelling in Russia is not expensive, the first-class fare from Nijni Novgorod to Perm, a four days' journey, being only 36s.

'Those who have hitherto written of journeys to Siberia have told of a dismal drive from Perm to Ekaterineburg; but this misfortune did not fall to our lot, since in the autumn of 1878 a railway was opened over the mountains, and the journey is now accomplished in about four-and-twenty hours. The distance is 312 miles, and between the two termini are about 30 stations.*

---

* Of the three divisions, the Northern or barren Ural, as the Russians call it, beginning at the source of the Pechora, is the most elevated and the least known. The Southern Ural begins about midway between Perm and Orenburg, and descends to the banks of the Ural river. It is a pastoral country, and about 100 miles in width. The range is here less than 3000 feet in height. The Central Ural may be considered as a wide undulation, beginning on the west on the banks of the Kama. Perm, situated on the right bank of the river, is 378 feet above the sea level, and on the post road to Ekaterineburg the highest point is 1,633 feet, which, if my reckoning is correct, is 40 feet less than the highest station on the railway. I set my aneroid at Perm, and found that at the fourth station, Seleenka, a distance of 172 miles, we had mounted 470 feet ; the next 22 miles brought us down again to 120 feet, after which for 60 miles we continued to ascend to Bisir, which registered 1,300 feet above Perm, and was the highest station on the road. Level ground succeeded for about 30 miles to the border station, after which in 50 miles we descended 750 feet to Shaltanka, 10 miles beyond which we had remounted 200 feet ; and on this level we kept to Iset, the last station but one. The road then descended about 150 feet to Ekaterineburg, which is said to be 858 feet above the sea level.

'From the prominence given in maps of Europe to the Ural chain, one is apt from childhood to expect something grand. The entire length of the range, including its continuation in Novaia Zemlia, is about 1,700 miles. Its highest peak, however, does not attain to more than 6000 feet, and many parts of the range are not more than 2000 feet above the sea level. No part of it is permanently covered with snow. Travellers by the old route describe, in passing it, a never-failing object of interest on the frontier in the shape of a stone, on one side of which is written "Europe" and on the other "Asia," across which, of course, an English boy could stride, and announce that he had stood in two quarters of the globe at once. Travellers by the new route miss this opportunity; but they have its equivalent in three border stations, one of which is called "*Europa*," the next "*Ural*," and the third "*Asia*," through which those who have journeyed can say what no other travellers can, that they have passed by rail from one quarter of the globe into another.'

I have, in a preceding chapter, brought forward accounts of the floral beauty and forest character of the country. No less interesting accounts have been given of the social intercourse and luxurious living to be enjoyed in Ekaterineburg. Some of the accounts of this given by visitors have savoured more of animal than intellectual enjoyment; but even this is not in keeping with the views generally entertained in regard to life in Siberia. My deceased friend, Mr Wilkinson, gives yet another peep into life here.

There is a monastery in Ekaterineburg which is of some fame in that region, and deservedly so. My friend, writing to me of a visit which he made to it, told:—'We have heard a great deal of the dead weight of innumerable drones and non-producers hanging like a millstone on the neck of Russia, a vast army, consisting of monks and nuns, and chinovnicks great and small, &c., &c. There are said to be eight or nine millions residing in monasteries alone; and yet besides these, apparently you meet with

begging nuns and lazy monks all over Russia; still I think
the figure must be overstated. However, if all the monastic establishments were like the one in Ekaterineburg,
they are not only deserving of toleration but of all praise
and encouragement, for it is nothing more nor less than a
reformatory, industrial, and educational home. I had not
been long in Ekaterineburg before I was told I ought to
pay my devoir to the lady abbess at the nunnery. The
following Easter I embraced the opportunity, sent in my
card, and was soon ushered into a large, light, well
furnished suite of rooms ; but quite monastic in their style.
There was a freezing depression about it. The doors,
walls, blinds, table-cloths, furniture covers, all white as
snow, but no curtains, and few carpets. There was a
freezing depression about it, but I was not long left to
pursue my reveries alone. I soon heard that there was
life and joyousness even in a nunnery, as a young bouyant
nun came skipping and humming through the rooms, but
when she caught a glance of me she immediately threw
herself into the regulation slow, demure carriage ; bent
herself into a right angle as she bowed, and passed on for
the head-dress and veil of the lady superior, that had
been inadvertently left on the table. By-and-by I soon
heard the measured stately tread as of a procession. I
rose as the old lady was led in between two senior sisters,
secretary and treasurer of the establishment.

'They all bowed very low, I did the same, when the
mother stepped forward, offered me her hand, and we kept
bowing so long, with such low revential inflections, that I
was afraid our heads would come into collision.

'I then had the honour to *Chreepto se Vatsia*, inter-
changing salutations with the venerable lady, kissing three
times orthodox fashion. She then politely invited me to
be seated, thanked me for the unexpected pleasure of my
visit. Tea and lemon was served, then wines and *zakusky*.
Capital institution that of Russia, handing the cup that
cheers but not inebriates, at every hour of the day. They
will not let you go out as you come in ; and what can be

nicer than that delicious beverage to help the genial flow
of conversation. We chatted and sipped our tea, she asking
a great many questions about our English customs, church
holidays, &c. ; begged that I would repeat the visit now that
we were no longer strangers ; professed a great admiration
for the English; believes them to be a religious, philan-
thropic, and missionary people; knows all about our
various societies and voluntary contributions, &c., &c. I
then took my leave, thinking I had seen the last of the
abbess of Ekaterineburg till next Easter; but most
wonderful to say before the holidays are over up comes
driving to my door a carriage and four, with out riders, when
Mother Matrony is announced. Of course "at home." I
was quite a lion after, as she never returns the visit of
any but the Bishop, though all the nobility and gentry of
the town consider themselves bound to pay court at the
palace of the lady abbess. She has the highest rank of
any bishop or general in Ekaterineburg, and is always
visited by any of the Imperial family passing through
Ekaterineburg. I shortly accepted the invitation to go
and see the monastery; when she personally conducted me
through the whole establishment. I was much struck
with the order, cleanliness, and industry that pervaded the
whole place. She conducts a very large and profitable
business in wax candles, from the tall and highly em-
bellished church mould to the tiniest taper. I thought—
this is a business I could dispense with ; then I thought
these poor girls had better be making church candles than
doing nothing, or worse ; and I thought if I can't worship
with a candle what right have I to quarrel with those
that can't worship without. I thought much better have
too much ritual than none at all. A shrewd, clever old
lady that ! She pointed with great pride to the church
paintings and decorations, all done by her own daughters,
and when she asked me what I thought about them I
was rather in a fix. " Well," I said, " they are not from
the pencil of Rosa Bonheur nor Angilicia Kaufman, but
they are very fair, considering who have done them—a

little too highly coloured perhaps." She borrowed from me the *Life of Christ* and other books. The idea of nuns copying subjects from Raphael ! The grounds, cemetery, and large cabbage and flower gardens, are all kept in nice prim order by the nuns; so they had something else to do besides pray. I stopped to service; but I would rather hear the chanting of the monks at Nevsky monastery than that of the nuns of Ekaterineburg. They do try the contralto, but there are too many squeaking trebles amongst them to make good harmony. There was nothing I disliked about the whole house excepting the obsequious, servile manner in which the principals in each department had to come and kiss her hand on presenting themselves; but she is highly spoken of as being remarkably kind, patient, and forbearing; and I have no doubt she had plenty of exercise for those Christian virtues in such a large community. All had a healthy, happy look about them. The bread, fish, and vegetables were all sweet and good, without stint or measure. Everything they wear is home-made, and excellent bootmakers they are, besides making fancy work of every kind for sale. She is open to receive any orphan, homeless wanderer, or repentant madeleine. She has upwards of 700 souls in her establishment, and she is rapidly extending the institution, in her own way doing a very good work. Never shall I forget the polite and courteous kindness of the lady abbess of Ekaterineburg.'

In Russia we meet with an institution in full vigour, which is gradually disappearing, if it has not entirely disappeared, from our own country. I refer to that of fairs. The great fair of Nijni Novgorod is still one of the wonders of the world.

Amongst others still famous is that of Irbit in the Ural, on the northernmost route by which Siberia is entered from Russia. It is held annually during the whole month of February, commencing on the first day of the month, and being closed by the 1st of March.

Of this my friend and correspondent, Mr Wilkinson, wrote to me :—

'I had heard a good deal about Irbit and of the Asiatics, and the number of interesting things to be found there ; but " Blessed is he that expecteth nothing, for he shall not be disappointed." Evidently I had expected too much, for I was much disappointed, if not disgusted. You do find there a few Chinamen, Persians, Armenians, Bokharians, &c., but they are few in number, are lost in the mass, and when encountered, they look as much out of their element as fish out of water. The chief business is done by Tartar and Siberian merchants. The greatest trade done there is in tea brought overland from Kiachta. Of packages of tea there are row after row, and pile upon pile—I am afraid now to say how many hundred thousand poods ; I think it was three—pure China tea, for which you must pay double the price in retail, and find it not so good, because mixed with the Canton and Indian teas. I have heard of tea sold there at 300 roubles a pound, but I have never seen or tasted tea of a higher price than 50 roubles. You find there also cotton, wool, madder, &c., from Bokhara and the steppes, but not in such quantities as you might expect. There is a good trade done in furs, in skins, and in fish. Heaps upon heaps of these delicious Siberian fish, seven and eight feet long, and five poods in weight ; and shoubes at all prices from 50 to 5000 roubles. But the principal articles are prints and fancy goods, iron and cutlery, taken there to meet the traders in the steppes, in Siberia, and the Ural. Haberdashery and drapery alone were said to be sold to the amount of 8,000,000 roubles.

'How do you think they carry on this trade ? The buyer must first pay off last year's bills, and settle old accounts if he can ; then he gets a fresh stock of goods on twelve, twenty-four, and sometimes thirty-six months' bills, as the Russian manufacturers must sell all off on such terms as they can. It won't do either to bring the goods back or to let them remain there till the following year. The Government and other banks are there also doing business on the same footing—viz., lading and teaming, cashing and discounting, receiving with one hand,

paying back with the other. Of course, there are failures
and liquidations every year, as there are sure to be on such
a rotten foundation as that—all on credit—and all trading
on Government money, which consists also of bills of credit.
The wholesale merchants and manufacturers from Moscow
and the surrounding district put on 15 and 20 per cent. per
annum for this long credit. The retailer makes systematically
a compound with his creditors about every five or six years,
after getting all in order for this. And this seems to be
an established and understood thing among them.

'During the fair there are said to be in Irbit at one time
from 200,000 to 300,000 people—that is why lodgings are so
dear, from 50 to 250 roubles a month. At other times
there are only about 7000 inhabitants. There are no
hotels, but there are several restaurants—the Exchange
gostinistya, or restaurant, has a good *menu*, but there is
an abominable feature about all of them, the least said
about which the better. In fact, all yarmokies which I
have seen, except Troitsk—and Nijni more than any of
them, are just a den of infamy, and a sink of iniquity,
without any effort at concealment. The roads to Irbit,
after you leave the Siberian track at Wamaskloff, are
something execrable—over vast drifts of snow on the open
plains, which are worn into deep hollows, one after another
in close succession, by the great amount of sledges passing
over them night and day without intermission for two
months before the fair ; so that, as you are dragged over
these, trenches, I call them, you go jolting and rocking up
and down, from side to side, like being in a chopping sea,
and experience the same unpleasant sensation, only in a
worse and aggravated form ; and this from year to year, without any attempt being made by anybody towards ameliorating the intolerable misery that everybody is growling
about. After the fair is over, if you return, you do find
a man or two here and there pattering and shuffling about
on the road, but as they say themselves, "One man on a
plain is not a battle."

'Mention has been made of the fair at Troitsk. Troitsk

fair is the very reverse of this every way in June and July. In the first place, you go bowling merrily along over good, hard, dry roads, on a sandy soil, at the rate of sixteen or eighteen versts an hour. I have often done a stage of twenty - five versts in seventy-five minutes, and without the usual accompaniments of jerks and jolts which you would think were going to dislocate every bone in your body. It is one of the most delightful journeys I ever made, through a very pretty and interesting country of iron and copper mines, marble works and gold washings, corn fields and pasture lands, interpersed here and there with woods of almost every kind, except the pine family.

' The Menobou Dbops, which means Court of Exchange, covers a vast area on the steppe, but it does not do anything like the amount of business it once did. Railways will knock all these yarmokies on the head in the long run, I suppose. It was very interesting to watch their long trains of camels bringing in the cotton, &c., from Yashkend, Khokand, Keia, Samarcand, Bokhara, &c., besides hundreds of yokes of oxen bringing in the wool, salt, &c., in clumsy, creaking, Asiatic carts from the Kerghis steppes. You wonder where are all the merchants, and where is all the business done, but as you pass round you find a group of five or six in a ring, on every spot, all cross-legged. Perhaps one is turning goods slowly and carefully over, layer after layer, as if they wanted to spin the job out as long as they could, barely raising their eyes or deigning to look till you are gone past. Then there is a whispered buzz of enquiry to know if you are bringing any fish to their net.

' Troitsk is on the border of that vast sea of sand called a steppe. It is a quiet unassuming town, because of the predominence of those peaceful sober Mahommedans. There are five *mechets* there—all little shabby tumble-down wooden buildings—*babagans* I call them, only those on the plain here are a great deal handsomer. The Tartars are all either very mean or very poor—a bit of both, I think. I have seen several grand Mahommedan edifices which they have begun to build, and were not able to finish. They don't worship and honour either their Allah or their Prophet much with their pockets. But of all the bare and wretched poverty I have ever seen, as you pass through the Tartar and Kalmuck villages, it beats all. And yet there are plenty of rich merchants among them; but they have all quite a propensity for petty pedling in preference to hard work. The first time I heard their muezzins calling out from those tall and slender minarets the summons to prayer, I enquired of a Tartar gentleman I was with, what it all amounted to, and he replied with great gravity, "Allah is great and good. Allah is one, and Mahomet is his Prophet. Haste all ye faithful to his temple, and worship before him!" And they well and willingly obey the call; for while that trumpet voice resounds far and wide you will see them hurrying from all parts, some even running from fear of being too late. I wonder how many of us run for fear of being too late for the first offering of praise and prayer? They have a reverend patriarchial look about them in their long flowing green kholats, ponderous snow-white turbans, and soft green embroidered boots. As soon as they are all assembled, and that human bell ceases to ring, you immediately see another remarkable scene. All the streets are again astir, but this time it is with the veiled wives and daughters of the devotees, paying their flying gossipping visits, while their husbands and fathers are at prayer, on rude conveyances very like what you see *lomovoi isvoschiks* have here, only lighter, with a board, a carpet, and a cushion thrown on the top. The veils are only shawls or large handkerchiefs worn over the top of their fur caps. The old and not very nice make no attempt at concealment, but the young and would-be beauty, fat, fair, and fifteen, after taking a good peep at you through the opening of her guady shawl, generally finds some excuse for throwing it open as she is passing you, while she pretends to rectify some part of her attire, affecting not to see you: she does not display her Tartaric charms, but she invites notice. They are not very elegant, those Tartar ladies, with their legs dangling over one side of their black four-wheeled bier. As the Irishman said when he was in a sedan without a bottom—"If it were not for the honour of riding, I should prefer walking."

'One day I was glad to have an invitation to tea with a Mahommedan gentleman from Bokara; for you may depend upon it that amongst these Asiatics you find more true gentility, genuine courtesy, politeness, and refinement of manners, than you do among all the tailor-made snobs and swells in London and Paris put together. The house was rather stuffy and stifling in its looks, as there were so many eider down pillows about. The lady of the house and her daughter, after a shaking of hands, went and stood near the door, just inside the drawing-room, dressed in rich silk velvets, lined and trimmed with the sable fur, the best of beaver caps, and long lace veils down to their heels. They then bowed and retired, but shortly reappeared in another costume of another colour, but equally extravagant in costliness; and this was done I don't know how many times, till all their best finery was shown off, I suppose. But their hospitality was overwhelming, even sickening—what with fruits, jams, confectionery, nuts, and what not, served up in honey. All you have to do, if you would please your host, is to eat and drink, and drink and eat incessantly; but no wines, nothing but delicious tea and coffee. I had the impertinence to ask the gentleman how many wives he had, or might have? "Might have four; had only one. Many of us have only one now—better one than more." "Indeed, why?" "Well, when you have one wife her fingers are hooked, and she sticks to your money, but when you have above one they have all got straight, open hands; it is nobody's interest to hold fast. They won't save for one another; they all try to cost you as much as they can. So all your money slips right through, and there is none left for the children." I am afraid this Mahommedan was

M

not the only man whose conjugal affection was governed by selfishness.

'I went one evening to see their worship. I was told I might stand in the porch where they leave their outer shoes, but on no account must I dare to defile their inner court of prayer. I thought of that passage in the history of Moses—"Draw not nigh hither; put off thy shoes from off thy feet, for where thou standest is holy ground." Very slow and solemn were those prayers, commencing at the door, all on their knees in straight, uniform rows; then at a signal from the mollah, they all rise, bow, and advance a few steps farther, then fall down prostrate to the floor, and so on up to the altar, such as it is. It reminded me of the passage, "O come let us worship and fall down and kneel before the Lord our Maker." And I asked myself whether we Nonconformists have not too little devotion and worship in our services, and whether our lazy, slovenly way of sitting and lolling in our pews during prayers offered to the Deity be not an insult to the Divine Majesty of our Lord and Master. We dare not serve our employers so, much less our Queen. It was a very quiet service—still enough to suit even the Quakers. No singing; a few passages from the Alcoran, droned by the mollah; then all hurried back to their homes and their business. And this is done five times a day. Once a week is enough, and too much, for some of us.

'On the outskirts of the town, on the bank of the river, is a fine long boulevard, commanding an extensive view of the plain, the *yarmonka*, and the motley crew of caravans and Asiatics there. There is a good orchestra playing in the pavilion every evening. The aristocracy, the Cossack officers, and the Russian officials, are all there with their families promenading about. But those stolid, imperturbable Mahommedans sit there cross-legged on the grass plots among the trees the whole evening talking stock, as if they grew there. I should like to have known their thoughts. About nine o'clock they shamble off to their own quarter of the town; which after that is as still as death—not a *kabac* or a drunken man to be seen. No Sir Wilfrid Lawson's Permissive Bill required here; but that is because they are not Christians, I suppose.

'I never saw handsomer, more athletic looking men than those Bokharians and Central Asians—perfect Adonises every one of them, proud and noble in mein and bearing, especially when mounted. They say they can do anything on a horse, but nothing off. Well, you won't catch them at hard work certainly. And it is no exaggeration to say that their piercing black eyes sparkle like diamonds; but the Baskirs, the Kalmuks, and the Kerghis, are poor, miserable, repulsive-looking beings—the very quintessence of Mongolian ugliness.

'I saw another, to me, very exciting scene. As I learned I should be some time in Troitsk, I went to the police office to send home a copy of my passport; but I found it was not a police office at all, as Troitsk is under a military commander of the Orenburg Kossae province. While waiting there a great commotion occurred in the street—people running, drums beating, soldiers marching—and while I was looking through the window all vanished out of the hall, and I was left alone. I, too, made a speedy exit, as I thought there must be a fire. I enquired from my *isvoschik* (driver) what it all meant. He said, "Follow on, and then you will see." I did so, and soon came up to the crowd, who were swarming round a tumbrel waggon. On an elevated platform was a young woman, sitting with her back to the horses, and her face to the merry, laughing, eager throng. Her screams were drowned by the rataplan of the drums, as well they might be, for she was weeping and writhing most piteously; but she was securely strapped back, arms, and feet. When we arrived at the echafote all was hushed as she was taken down and chained to a pillar in the centre, the military authorities

standing all round.   After the executioner had made all
ready, he rolled up his red shirt-sleeves (his face redder
than his shirt), threw a white towel over his shoulder,
drained off a tumbler of liquid fire, and took the murderous
looking whip in his hand.   The chief officer then read her
sentence, which I could not hear, she looking calm and
pale as a corpse.   A priest then advanced and confessed
her, waving the cross several times over her head.   As
soon as Jack Ketch prepared to strike the first blow, he was
stopped by the military commander, who read out a
commutation of her sentence to transportation to Siberia.
I felt thankful that both she and I were spared the torture, but there was a hum of dissatisfaction running
through the mob as the poor swooning creature was taken
down and tumbled into the cart and straw.   They had
been cheated out of the fun.   She had been condemned
for child murder, they said.   I then drove back to finish
my business, but nobody turned up, and I immediately
heard the drums beating again, and I saw two convicts
being borne off this time; but I had had enough, and
thought I must wait here.   I had not waited long before
the executioner was brought in bound.   It appeared that
he had no sooner begun to flog one of these poor culprits,
who was condemned to receive eighty lashes, because he
had escaped from Siberia—not the first time either—when
he was discovered picking something up from the stage,
which turned out to be a letter containing three roubles,
begging of him to use the instrument of torture as ten-
derly as possible : consequently the execution was stopped.
Such a flagrant act of dishonesty as that must be visited
with condign punishment !   As the man was led off in
irons to be sent back to the Governor of Orenburg,
I thought how these men strain at a gnat when they
can swallow a camel.

'I have often been asked about the climate up there.
Well, I myself asked that question of a German when I
first went to Ekaterineburg. He answered, " I will tell you

what my father always said in reply to that question ; he said there are eight months winter uninterrupedly, that was a settled thing, then two months spring, and two months autumn, all the rest are summer." That is a little exaggerated. I found it almost invariably two months only without frost, more or less. You can't set out your annuals before the 15th of June. I have had them all frozen up on the 25th of June ; and once during my residence there there was a heavy fall of snow on the 5th of July, and two men found frozen in a brick shed not far from my house—having lain down drunken no doubt overnight. The cold temperature ranges about from 15° to 25° Reaumour, and sometimes 35° and 41°, but not often nor long, though I have seen mercury beaten on the anvil like lead. In the summer, when the wind is southeast, it is nearly stifling. In the spring I have seen the mosquitoes in clouds hanging over the woods. The only protection to the skin is turpentine or smoke, so you have to decide which you can best endure—stink or stings.'

CHAPTER X.

LABOURING POPULATION.

IT may have been observed that in the mention made of concessions given to the enterprising men by whom the mining and metallurgical operations of the district were developed, there are included, besides forests and water power, lands and serfs. This was in accordance with what before the emancipation of the serfs was customary in Russia. Workmen were as necessary to the accomplishment of the enterprise as were ores and metals, and firewood and motive power. And the serfs being bound to the estates, workmen were provided by concessions of estates with a number of serfs upon them. In such circumstances the serfs might be of more value to the enterprising engineer than was the land. But they could not be purchased as might be slaves elsewhere.

An Englishman resident in Russia, whom I knew well, had a manufactory of white lead, which was deadly in its effects upon the workmen, and he frequently required to replace those whom he employed in the works. It was said of him that to do this he arranged with some landed proprietor to purchase a small strip of his property—if possible one comparatively densely peopled. Having done so, the serfs were his to employ them as he chose. Having drafted them off to his works, he had no further use for the land, and he made the original holder welcome to resume the use, if not also formal possession, of this. Let it not be forgotten that he was an Englishman !

There are sometimes seen gleams of light in the darkest sky, and gleams of humour in the saddest scenes. I was told, if I recollect aright, by his son, that on one occasion he was able to trace a robbery of his hen roost to one of his serfs ; and he had the man brought before him and charged with the crime. When asked by his owner, who was not in private life a very cruel man, 'Ivan, Ivano-vitch, did you kill that hen?' To the surprise of all, and the discomfiture of the sternness of his interrogator, the man replied, with a look and tone which implied that he expected ready approval of what he had done, 'Yes, Baron.' 'You have done very wrong Ivan, Ivanovitch,' said his owner with all gravity, 'You have stolen it and eaten it ; it was very wrong to do so.' 'No, Baron,' was the rejoinder, in a tone of surprise and offended innocence, which made it impossible to tell whether the man was a rogue or a fool, 'It is still your property ; it was yours, and I am yours you know ; so it is still yours.' Well, the man who was doomed to deadly work, though he did not know it, might be allowed to have his joke !

By such concessions as have been referred to, a supply of workmen was provided when the mining and metallur-gical works of the district were originated. And as these works are not necessarily very deadly, their children and descendants also supplied workmen for the works. Now it is otherwise. The estates remain the property of the barons ; but not so the serfs. Even then a serf might obtain permission from his baron to leave the estate for years, and work elsewhere, on payment of what was called *obrok*, an annual payment varying in amount with the probable earnings of the serf, and ranging from one pound to three hundred, the serf being liable to have his leave of absence recalled at any time. And of this national usage serfs from other estates may have availed themselves, and found employment in the mines and works.

Now, though serfdom has been abolished, the native labouring population of the district having been employed in these works for successive generations, they probably constitute the great bulk of the men employed. But

there, as in other parts of the Empire, men from a
distance may come and get employment for a week, a month,
a year, free to come, free to go, excepting in so far as
they may bind themselves by contract; and ready enough
to avail themselves of this freedom, they acquire without difficulty some knowledge of, and expertness in, the
little required of each to do—for the Russian peasant is
in many cases an imitative being—and with this knowledge and experience they may expect to get somewhat
higher wages from another employer.

I have great admiration for the emancipators of the
serfs, and full sympathy with the emancipated.   But from
what I know I think it not improbable that that measure,
one of justice to the serf, may have had not a little to do
with the present depression of the works here.

Of the peasantry in Siberia, Barry says : ' The peasants
of Siberia are found to be more civilised and better educated than those of the other parts of Russia;' and he
adds, ' this is doubtless due to the influence of the political
exiles who, from time to time, have been sent from the
centres of civilisation ·to live among them, and many of
whom, having no business to ·occupy them, spend their
time in the charitable occupation of teaching the children
of the peasantry in their neighbourhoods.

' The peasantry of Siberia are cleaner and better dressed
—altogether a finer class of men—than the peasants of
other parts. They seem to talk and express their opinions
with more freedom from restraint, and also to be better
informed of what is passing in the world than their
countrymen further south. Altogether, they seem to have
been more liberally educated and trained, and the traveller
cannot fail to be struck with the improvement he must
notice in the general condition and appearance of the
people as he advances further north towards the Siberian
deserts.

' The rise of the scale of civilisation in Siberia is indicated, amongst other ways, by the improved condition·of

the females of the population. In Central Russia the women are treated, as all uncivilised people treat women, with neglect and tyranny. She is left to do the hard work, and slave at field labour, while her lord and master alternates the amusement of drinking and sleeping. . . . Now, in Siberia, this evidence of barbarism is not so prominent. There the woman takes her proper place, looking after her household and her children, whilst the man attends to his proper duties also.'

' But what of the exiles?' I hear some one say. ' What of *the exiles of Siberia*, of whose sufferings we, in the days of our youth, and our fathers before us, and our fathers' fathers, have read with deep interest and sympathy and tears—what of them?' To see them we must go further afield. Siberia is a wide word. When a traveller from Europe reaches the summit of the Urals 'there stretches far before him,' says Dr Lansdell, 'a region known as Russia in Asia, the dimensions of which are very hard for the mind to realise. It measures 4000 miles from east to west, about 2000 from north to south, and covers nearly five and three-quarter millions of square miles. It is larger by two millions of square miles than the whole of Europe ; about twice as big as Australia, and nearly one hundred times as large as England.'

All this is Siberia; and the mines to which the exiles are sent lie further to the east, and the more remote of them thousands of miles away towards the rising sun. But we are on the border land of Siberia, and in a position from which something may be learned of them.

Herbert Barry, formerly director of the Chapeloffsky estates and iron works in the Government of Vladimir, Tamboff, and Nijni Novgorod, and author of a work entitled *Russian Metallurgical Works*, already cited, and another work entitled *Russia in* 1870, writes in regard in exiles in Siberia :—

' There are two distinct classes of detenus—criminal prisoners and political exiles—and these again are sub-

divided into several divisions. First, as to the criminal
prisoners. The worst culprits only are sent to work in
the mines—mostly in the silver mines of the Nerchinsk
district. As these are always the worst sort of criminals,
guilty of murder or other similar crimes, and as the work
in the mines is not particularly hard nor injurious to
health, and as, moreover, all the people working in the
mines now live above ground, they may be considered a
good deal better off than they deserve to be. . . .

  ' We hang our murderers ; the French guillotine theirs ;
the Russians, more wisely and humanely, in my opinion,
use theirs for certain kinds of labour, and take the greatest
care of their health.

  '·Another class of criminals are those sent to various
kinds of forced labour above ground ; and the remainder
are only exiled to certain spots where they are obliged to
live under the surveillance of the police : formed into
little colonies among themselves. I have never heard
any reason why the Russians should be said to treat their
criminals worse than other nations.

  ' As to political offenders, they are subject to no further
punishment than is involved in their compulsory residence
within a certain distance of some given centre. So long
as they do not go beyond their alloted circle they are in
all other respects perfectly free. Many among them have
entered the employment of Government entirely of their
own accord. Many of them also are now in a better position in Siberia than they would be in their own country,
and have no wish to return home. Some, on the other
hand, are in indifferent circumstances. One miner told
me lately that in his works he was employing two men
who had been colonels in the army at 80 kopecs a day for
each [at that time from two shillings to two shillings and
eightpence—say half-a-crown sterling]. I do not believe
that there is one instance of a political exile, properly so-
called, working in the mines, or doing any other kind of
forced work for Government account.

  ' It has been too common a custom to mix up some of

the criminals with political prisoners, in speaking of these. So you may hear that a certain prisoner is a "political," and on going carefully into his case you will find that although the man may have been mixed up with politics in some way or another, yet he was sent to Siberia for some crime quite distinct from his political tendencies.

'I âm not,' says he, 'giving my own opinion only, which, like that of other travellers, is very liable to error; but I am speaking the opinions of men educated and living on the spot, honest in their opinions, and well able to judge; and I think it only honest, as I have had unusual opportunities of collecting information on the subject, to record what I have heard and seen.

'It is not my business to justify the act of banishing men from their homes, often for a mere expression of opinion. Their lot is doubtless unhappy enough, in the mere fact of their exile from all that is near or dear to them. It does not need to be painted in blacker colours than the truth will justify, nor exaggerated by false statements of cruelties and sufferings which do not exist.'

'Of late years,' says he again, 'a great improvement has been made in the means of transporting prisoners of all kinds to their destinations. Formerly they walked on foot the whole distance, and months were consumed on the journey, and many fell victims to the fatigue. Now steamers carry them to Perm, and from Perm they are sent on to their destination by carriages. So carefully are they looked after now that in winter they do not travel on the roads. . . .

'Five years is the shortest term of punishment. The worst kind of criminals have their head shaved, some on one side only, and some all over.'

A different account of the treatment to which noble exiles, banished to Siberia in the beginning of the reign of Nicholas, and their noble wives were subjected, is given by Atkinson in his volume entitled, *Travels in the Regions of the Upper and Lower Amoor;* and statements similar to

those made by him were made to me when resident in St.
Petersburg, at the time I have stated, when, as I have also
stated, I had the gratification of meeting with one of those
noble women who had voluntarily shared the exile of her
husband and her sons, and only returned after their death.
My opinion is that both accounts are substantially correct;
that of Barry and of others accordant therewith, not less
than that which Atkinson has given; and I find no difficulty in recording them as statements of facts.

The statements of Barry are in accordance with general
impressions which I received while resident in St. Petersburg from 1833 to 1840, in the reign of Nicholas. At that
time I heard the common gossip of the day; and from this I
received my impressions. Beyond this occasionally information reached me incidentally and unsought through
different channels; but my opportunities of forming an
independent opinion of any value were few. The treatment to which exiles, whom I knew after their return to
Russia, had been subjected in Siberia, was never a subject of conversation between us; and what I did learn of
this was from others more intimately acquainted with
them or their connections. I had something to do with
supplying the exiles with New Testaments, but this never
brought me into personal contact with exiles; and only into
indirect communication with exiles setting out on their
weary journey.

Though the Russian Bible Society was virtually
suppressed, the Scriptures were allowed to be sold as
before. In the year 1828 two benevolent ladies in England suggested the propriety of supplying the Holy Scriptures to such of the exiles banished to Siberia as might be
able to read. They offered to contribute annually towards
the expense of the supply, and wrote to St. Petersburg to
Mr John Venning, who was a member of the committee
appointed to superintend the discipline of prisons, re-
questing him to undertake the distribution of the books

amongst those for whom they were intended. Mr Venning
acceded at once to their request; and when he found it
necessary to return to England, Dr Haas, of Moscow,
kindly undertook the work. And it was then found that
Moscow was a much better place than St. Petersburg for
carrying out the benevolent suggestion. In a few years
after this a sufficient number of New Testaments were
placed at the disposal of Dr Haas to enable him to give a
copy to every criminal passing through Moscow, the
number of which must have been very great, as to that
city prisoners were sent from twenty-two of the Governments of Russia, that they may be conveyed thence to the
various penal settlements in the interior. Dr Haas was
afterwards permitted to extend the boon to a numerous
class of persons attached to the convoys, to facilitate the
distribution of the daily allowance of Government for the
support of the criminals while pursuing their journey.
These were chiefly discharged soldiers. They were neither
exiles nor prisoners, and they often envied the poor exiles
the copy of the Scriptures granted to these, but not to
them. And it soon appeared that if they could be procured, many copies might be satisfactorily disposed of
amongst these outcasts of society, and through them conveyed to various and distant parts of the Empire.

Dr Haas was a Roman Catholic, but he took a deep
interest in the circulation of the sacred volume. He was
at the head of the prison discipline committee of Moscow,
and his situation supplied him with many opportunities
of ameliorating the spiritual condition of the wretched
men going into exile. He had frequent interviews with
them, while they were in confinement, and they had all to
pass in review before him, as they set out on their long
and toilsome journey. He availed himself of that opportunity to present them with a copy of the New Testament, seeing, himself, that it was entered in their little
inventory of stores, that the officer in charge might be
made responsible for its being delivered to them again on

their reaching their destination. He then addressed to each of them a few words of exhortation and counsel.*

All of the copies thus distributed by Dr Haas during seven years which I spent in St. Petersburg, passed through my hands as the unpaid agent of the British and Foreign Bible Society. But this gave me no opportunity for learning, by personal observation, the treatment to which the exiles in exile were subjected.

Dr Lansdell, however, has latterly travelled through the country from the Urals to the Amoor, personally distributing the Scriptures, and giving his attention specially to the condition of the exiles; and in his work, entitled *Through Siberia*, he has published his impressions and the observations on which they were founded.

In a lengthened notice of this work, which appeared in the *Scotsman* when it was published, it is stated:—

' The origin and the objects of the journey were somewhat unusual. Mr Lansdell, who is in "holy orders," has travelled in almost every part of Europe, visiting prisons and hospitals, and distributing copies of the Bible and other religious books. A lady friend in Finland reminded him that Siberia was a fine field for this kind of mission work. " Parson Lansdell," she wrote, " do you go to Siberia; " and, like a true knight-errant, with the aid of funds supplied by a " generous friend," he at once set his face for Tobolsk. His friends all assured him that there was no chance of the Siberian authorities allowing him

---

* Nor was it the poor and the prisoner alone whose good he endeavoured to promote. His desire seemed to be ' as he had opportunity, to do good unto all men.' The late Emperor Alexander II., when heir-apparent, visited the public institutions of Moscow —the prisons amongst the rest. On that occasion Dr Haas had the honour of conducting his Highness through the different cells; and on leaving the dungeons in which great criminals were confined, he, in a solemn manner, said to him, ' May it please your Highness, there are four things which I urge every one leaving these cells to think of before it be too late :—Death, Judgment, Heaven, Hell.' Having accompanied the Grand Duke through the rest of the establishment, he led him into a small apartment in which he kept the New Testaments designed for distribution, and presenting to him a copy in Russ, one of those designed for the exiles, he said, ' In every other institution visited by your Highness you must have been presented with bread and salt ; allow me to present to you the Bread of Life.' The volume was graciously received, and handed by the Grand Duke to an aide-de-camp in attendance, with directions to take charge of it till they got home. A copy of the New Testament in French was, at the same time, presented to the page in waiting.

within their prison walls. In the event of his getting a glimpse of the interior of these convict establishments, he had steeled his mind to support the sight of the excruciating sufferings supposed to accompany Siberian exile. He was agreeably surprised to find that in neither respect were his expectations fulfilled. The prison authorities were most courteous and complacent in encouraging his evangelistic labours; and all that need be said of these is, that Mr Lansdell succeeded in accomplishing the object of his ambition, which was "to put at least a copy of the New Testament, or of the Gospels, in every room of every prison, and every ward of every hospital, throughout Siberia." At the same time, the widest facilities were given him of informing himself regarding the arrangement of the Siberian prisons. These institutions are far from being perfect; it is hardly in the nature of things that they should be. But no such "horrors" as certain English politicians and journals are accustomed to expatiate upon were to be seen. On the contrary, the great and characteristic fault of the Siberian prisons is the laxity of the discipline. Most of the "Russian barbarities" that are connected, in the popular mind, with the Siberian penal colonies refer to a day now long past, and, as Mr Lansdell says, are not more just, as a picture of the present condition of things in Russian prisons, than it would be a description of the pillory and ear-cropping as among the judicial punishments of England. Other stories are pure inventions, apparently set afloat to make political capital of. As an illustration of this, Mr Lansdell mentions the circumstantial account brought before Parliament by Mr Joseph Cowen, of the dreadful fate of "700 persons, mostly men and women of education, packed in the hold of a small ship," and despatched by sea from Odessa to Saghalien, "the service for the ordinary transportation of criminals to Siberia," as a London paper explained, "being already overtaxed." Of these unfortunates, it was said, "250 had died on board, 150 were landed in a dying state," &c. The facts are, as Mr

Lansdell shows, that the despatch of prisoners by the sea passage, instead of the overland route, was a humane measure of improvement, and that the large merchant steamer conveying the party in question arrived at Vladivostock a week or two before himself, the prisoners being all in excellent health, and not one death having occurred on the passage. He travelled by the "convict route" across Asia, and his companion returned by the same road, at the very time that the roads were said to be blocked with convoys of exiles; yet the whole number they met with, or definitely heard of, both in going and returning, did not, he thinks, amount to fifty. The fact is, that Siberian convicts are not, as a class, more deserving of sympathy than the occupants of any penal establishment at home; and it is generally the most desperate criminals that are sent to the far eastern settlements. Political prisoners are seldom to be seen in confinement. Mr Lansdell's impression is, that "the greater number of them go to prison only for a short time, or not at all, and are then placed in villages and towns, where they are expected to get their living. Looking at the political prisoners I saw in the separate rooms of the various prisons, at those with whom I came into personal contact, and those of whom mention was made as living in the towns through which I passed, I think, if I had been commissioned to give a soverign to each, fifty coins would have sufficed for the purpose." The statistics obtained seem to show that, of those banished, only one seventh are condemned to hard labour; and their educational status may be gathered from the fact that, at the prison of Tiumen, where the exiles are brought from Europe and distributed over Asia, out of 470 prisoners, only 42 could read and write well, and 386 were wholly illiterate. Summing up his experiences, Mr Lansdell says:—

'"I have met with deep and almost universal conviction that the prisons of Siberia, compared with those of other countries, are intolerably bad. This I cannot endorse. A proper comparison would be between the Russian sent to

Siberia and the English convict as formerly transported to Botany Bay ; but comparing the convicts of the two nations as they now are, and taking the three primary needs of life—clothing, food, and shelter—the Russian convict proves to be fed more abundantly, if not better, than the English convict, and the clothing of the two, having respect to the dress of their respective countries, is very similar. A convict's labour in Siberia is certainly lighter than in England ; he has more privileges; friends may see him oftener and bring him food ; and he passes his time, not in the seclusion of a cell, nor under imposed silence, but among his fellows, with whom he may lounge, talk, and smoke. I am now looking at things from a prisoner's point of view, and referring more especially to his animal requirements. When we look at his intellectual, moral, and religious nature, then it must be allowed my former comparsion, as between Russian and English prisons, no longer holds good."

'In these latter respects, he admits, the Russian system is sadly deficient; and one special hardship is, that the prisoner condemned to hard labour is robbed of Sunday rest. The Russian Criminal Code, while it has abolished capital punishment, except for murder, is not yet entirely purged of barbarous methods of punishment. The "knout" is no longer known, and Mr Lansdell found difficulty in getting a description of what it used to be like. The birch rod cannot be a formidable weapon, judging from the story told of a soldier who received 1100 lashes for theft, and at the end of a fortnight came to Mr Lansdell's host, from whom he had stolen the goods, to ask for a glass of grog, remarking that "for a bottleful he would not mind having another 1100, if it might again be followed by a fine time in hospital." But the *plete*, a whip of twisted hide, which, however, is only used at three prisons in Eastern Siberia, must be a very efficient substitute for the knout. Mr Lansdell did not see it in operation, but the description he gives of it should take away any hankering for a closer acquaintance with it. The taking

N

of the life of the criminal is simply at the discretion of the executioner who wields this murderous implement. It is used only in exceptional cases of incorrigibility—in fact, the prison director at Tiumen stated that, out of 80,000 exiles who had passed through his hands, only one had been flogged; and the doubtful excuse is offered for it that, as an escaped criminal knows he can commit half-a-dozen murders without danger of hanging, some other strong deterrent is needed to protect the inhabitants. This is not by any means a fanciful danger, as may be judged by this account of an approach to the penal colony of Kara, in the Trans-Baikal province :—

' " As we drove along and darkness crept on, there passed us labouring men, who saluted us. ' Who,' said I, ' are they?' ' They are convicts,' said the Colonel (the commandant of the colony.)   ' Convicts,' said I ; ' How then are they loose ?'   ' Oh,' said he, ' a large proportion of the condemned—perhaps half—live out of their prisons in their houses *en famille*.   But they ought not to be out after dark.'   I then began to inquire respecting the crimes of the prisoners, and was informed that there were in the place about 800 murderers, 400 robbers, and 700 vagrants, or *brodiagi* (a class mostly composed of convicts who have escaped and been recaptured) ; and having been told what proportion of these were loose, I was not surprised to hear the Colonel say he usually, if possible, avoided being out at night.   I approved of his caution." '

CHAPTER XI.

THE CONQUEST OF SIBERIA.

WHILE engrossed with matters pertaining to forestry, and matters of such interest as mines of iron, of copper, and of gold, it may not have occurred to some of my readers that we have got beyond what was at one time considered the boundary of Europe. Yet such is the case. The Ural mountains, throughout much of their extent, constitute this boundary, and here they constitute the boundary between Russia and Siberia. Even in Perm, the produce of the soil, and the nationality, language, and customs of the inhabitants, partake decidedly of an Asiatic character; but geographically it belongs to Russia.

The boundary consists of hills rather than mountains; the slope or inclination is slight, the elevations inconsiderable, and in many cases it appears more as a rolling, undulating country than even as a region of hills, and the traveller by the highway might fail to know when he had crossed the boundary line—but there stands at the spot an obelisk. It is a plain stone, with no other inscription than the word 'EUROPE' on one side and 'ASIA' on the other, and is said to have been erected in honour of Yermak, a Cossack robber chief, who, towards the end of the sixteenth century atoned for his crimes by discovering and partly conquering Siberia for the Russians.

'Yermak,' writes Michie, 'being outlawed, found his way, with some two hundred adventurers, across the Ural. After pillaging the Tartars for some time, his handful of troops, *i.e.*, robbers, became so wasted by constant fighting that he could no longer maintain himself amongst his numerous enemies. It then occurred to Yermak to return to Moscow, announce his discovery, and make his peace with the Tsar. The robber was promoted to the rank of a hero, and was appointed to command an expedition for the conquest of Siberia. Yermak first crossed the Ural in 1580, and in 1660 nearly all the Siberian tribes were subjugated by Russia.'

In regard to the mountain range, he says: 'I had formed great conceptions of this mountain chain, but the illusion was dispelled when, on inquiring for the Urals, I was pointed to dusky, wooded, undulating hills, in appearance not more imposing than the Lammermoor range in Scotland. I know not why thy are so darkly shaded on most of our maps, and made to look like a formidable barrier between the two continents. They certainly cover a broad expanse of country, but in elevation they are really insignificant, and rendered still more so in appearance by their very gradual rise from the level country. The elevation in the latitude of Ekaterineburg is little more than 2000 feet above the sea; and the plain on the Siberian side being between 800 and 1000 feet in elevation, the gentle slope of the mountains makes them look diminutive.'

Of the conquest of the country, Dr Lansdell tells:— 'It can hardly be said that Siberia was familiar to the Russians before the middle of the sixteenth century; for, although at an earlier period an expedition had penetrated as far as the Lower Obi, yet its effects were not permanent. Later, Ivan Vassilievitch II. sent a number of troops over the Urals, laid some of the Tartar tribes under tribute, and in 1558 assumed the title of " Lord of Siberia." Kutchum Khan, however, a lineal descendant of Genghis Khan, punished these tribes for their defection, and regained their fealty, and so ended again for a while the result of the Russian expedition. A third invasion, however, was made in a way quite unexpected. Ivan Vassilievitch II. had extended his conquests to the Caspian Sea, and opened commercial relations with Persia; but the merchants and caravans were frequently pillaged by hordes of banditti, called Don Cossacks, whom the Tsar attacked, killing some, and taking prisoner or scattering others. Among the dispersed were 6000 free-booters, under the command of a chief named Yermak Timofeeff, who made their way to the banks of the Kama, to a settlement at Orel, belonging to one of the Strog-anoffs, where they were entertained during a dreary winter, and where Yermak heard of an inviting field of adventure, lying on the other side of the Urals. Thither he determined to try his fortunes, and after an unsuccessful attempt in the summer of 1578, started again with 5000 men in June of the next year. It was eighteen months before he reached the small town of Tchingi, on the banks of the Tura; by which time his followers had dwindled down, by skirmishes, privation, and fatigue, to 1500 men. But they were all braves. Before them was Kutchum Khan, prince of the country, already in position, and, with numerous troops, resolved to defend himself to the last. When at length the two armies stood face to face, that of Yermak was further reduced to 500 men, nine-tenths of those who left Orel having perished. A desperate fight ensued, the Tartars were routed, and Yermak pushed on to Sibir, the residence of the Tartar princes. It was a small fortress on the banks of the Irtish, the ruins of which are still standing, and of which I have seen a photograph, if I mistake not, among Mr Seebohm's collection.

'Yermak was now suddenly transformed to a prince, but he had the good sense to see the precariousness of his grandeur, and it became plain that he must seek for assistance. He sent, therefore, fifty of his Cossacks to the Tsar of Muscovy, their chief being adroitly ordered to represent to the Court the progress which the Russian troops, under the command of Yermak, had made in Siberia, where an extensive empire had been conquered in the name of the Tsar. The Tsar took very kindly to this, pardoned Yermak, and sent him money and assistance. Reinforced by 500 Russians, Yermak multiplied his expeditions, extended his conquests, and was enabled to subdue various insurrections fomented by the conquered

Kutchum Khan.   In one of these expeditions he laid siege
to the fortress of Kullara, which still belonged to his foe,
and by whom it was so bravely defended that Yermak had
to retreat.   Kutchum Khan stealthily followed the Russians, and, finding them negligently posted on a small
island on the Itish, he forded the river, attacked them by
night, and came upon them so suddenly as with compara-
tive ease to cut them to pieces.   Yermak perished, but
not, it is said, by the sword of the enemy.   Having cut
his way to the water's edge, he tried to jump into a boat,
but, stepping short, he fell into the water, and the weight
of his armour carried him to the bottom.   Thus perished
Yermak Timofeeff, and when the news reached Sibir, the
remainder of his followers retired from the fortress, and
left the country.

'The Court of Moscow, however, sent a body of 300
men, who before long made a fresh incursion, and reached
Tchingi almost without opposition.   There they built the
fort of Tiumen, and re-established the Russian sovereignty.
Being soon afterwards reinforced, they extended their
operations, and built the fortresses of Tobolsk, Sungur,
and Tara, and soon gained for the Tsar all the territory
west of the Obi.   The stream of conquest then flowed
eastward apace.   Tomsk was founded in 1604, and became
the Russian head-quarters, whence the Cossacks organised
new expeditions.   Yeneseisk was founded in 1619, and,
eight years afterwards, Krasnoiarsk.   Passing the Yenesei,
they advanced to the shores of Lake Baikal, and
in 1620 attacked and partly conquered the populous nation of the Buriats.   Then, turning northwards
to the basin of the Lena, they founded Yakutsk in 1632,
and made subject, though not without considerable difficulty, the powerful nation of the Yakutes; after which
they crossed the Aldan mountains, and in 1639 reached
the Sea of Okhotsk.   Thus in the span of a single lifetime
—70 years—was added to the Russian crown a territory
as large as the whole of Europe, whose ancient capital, as
I have said, was Tobolsk.'